The Girl *that* Ran

Ruth Anthony-Obi

THE GIRL THAT RAN
Copyright © 2019 Ruth Anthony-Obi

ISBN: 9781098683214

Published by:
RMPublishers
Office 1, Izabella House
24-26 Regent Place
Birmingham
B1 3NJ
www.rm-pa.org
info@rm-pa.org

Dedication

I want to say a big thank you to my family who have all been very supportive over the years since I started writing on a piece of paper. Col Anthony Uzoma Obi, Chief Mrs Linda A.U Obi, and my dearest sister Belinda Obi. I love you all.

I would also like to dedicate my first work to God for he has kept me alive day after day. Not only that; it is him who gave me this humble talent and I pray that he will continually fill my mind with more things to write.

Prologue

'Help me!'

A man desperately cried out from a distance away from the peaceful village of Umi. The evening rain muddled his cries of help as people hurriedly sought shelter. Not deterred by their indifference, he ran faster until he reached a few people sheltered under a mango tree close to the town square. People noticed him immediately, and their curiosity was replaced with horror as they saw what he carried in his arms; the lifeless bodies of two children with foam covered mouths and greying skins. No one moved to help him even as he knelt in the rain weeping uncontrollably.

"Please help me! My sons... I just looked away for a few minutes and... they ingested poisonous plants...please save them I beg you," he implored as he gently placed them side by side on the wet ground.

The people began to snap their fingers maliciously at him while others judgementally whispered about him, but none attempted to help him. Finally, in the midst of all the chaos, an elder stepped forward and spat at the corpses of the young children.

"You are cursed... you are a doomed creature," the man exclaimed pointing accusing fingers at him.

A woman turned to him shivering as though the mere sight of him brought her bad dreams. "Was it not last week that he lost his wife and unborn child? He is not only cursed, he is also a bad omen that should be gone from our sacred village," she proclaimed to her avid listeners.

Without hesitation, the people who gathered began to throw dirt at him while screaming for his exit from their blessed village. The man remained motionless in his kneeling position, paralysed by their stark hatred of his person. This place was the town he had grown up in, the home of his parents, and land he had trodden upon as a child filled with so many hopes and dreams. Sorrowfully, he regarded his now dead sons before meeting the hateful gazes of people whom he had never done any wrong to. What had he ever done to them? Why was he despised so much?

His internalized agony was interrupted when he felt thick mud hurled at him; it stained his face and stung his eyes. He looked up searchingly as his whole being was overtaken by rage. Without wasting another moment, he blindly rushed towards the culprit forgetting his grief; soon a fight ensued. At that point, reasoning eluded him and all he wanted was to feed them with all the anger that he felt towards them.

He struck the man continuously not caring about the pain in his knuckles or the fact that with each descend of his fist, the limb returned bloodier than before. People all around gathered him defensively as they attempted to dislodge him from the semi-conscious man, but in his moment of insanity; all he wanted was to hurt this unfortunate scapegoat, and to make him feel a fraction of all he felt. Suddenly in a painstaking moment, the man realised that he had been hit. The impact of his assault spread throughout the back of his head, and the man found himself losing this battle. For a big man, his fall was an easy tumble that sent him straight into unconscious darkness.

"What do we do with this vagabond?" asked one of the town's man as he discarded the log which was used to render their mutual enemy unconscious.

"Take him and his cursed offspring outside our town and leave them to the vultures. Fortune has smiled on us because this is killing two birds with one stone. He will finally die, and we will not have to tolerate him any

longer," scoffed the town's chief as he delegated the task of discarding the man and the dead bodies of his sons.

None of the people present on that day protested, and no one demanded justice for the grieving man. This very event served as a confirmation of why the man had always chosen to be alone because even now when he needed their sympathy; he would never receive it. Likened to the standard of trash, the man and his dead sons were lifted and discarded at the outskirts of town where the villagers hoped that wild animals would devour them.

The rain continued to beat, mud continued to cover their bodies and the town embedded in hate for this man, continued to exist.

1

The Rain...

Six Years Later

May

*D*alu had always appreciated the beauty in rainfall especially on a night such as this one when it poured like little drops of tears from the sky. It brought an aftermath of a chilly night combined with the earthy smell of the soil mixing with air. To him, this was the perfect blend that symbolized an end to the cleansing of the atmosphere. People assumed that the rain was just part of nature, a normal occurrence that was expected to happen at its given time, but he viewed it as an affirmation that even the earth had feelings when it allowed itself to shed tears for the people inhabiting it.

This particular night, along a muddied path in the outskirts of the village, emerged Dalu who was cautiously followed by three other people; two women sharing an umbrella and a man shielded in his raincoat. There was a noticeable distance between the small group and Dalu because none of them attempted to walk any closer to him than necessary.

Dalu did not fault them for their distance, after all, he was the town appointed lunatic in the little village of *Umi*. Firmly, he steadied the umbrella over his head, and walked in mechanical paces ignoring the soft earth beneath his bare feet. Repeatedly, because of his appearance, people were quick to judge him seeing as his lack of interest in the way he presented himself translated the message of a man too fed up with life to care. The truth was that Dalu was at the point where he could no longer comprehend what the essence of his existence on earth contributed. It was why he chose to become this empty shell of a man with his uncut hair hanging over his shoulders in dirty dreadlocks and an unkempt beard masking half of his expressionless face and throat. Due to the many hours spent under the sun planting crops to sustain him, his dark skin was sunburnt with uneven patches disappearing into his clothes. It did not help that on rare occasions when people encountered him, he was always dressed in unbefitting clothes and conversed with himself.

Believing that he was out of earshot, both women behind him began gossiping.

"How unfortunate we are to be walking in the same road as this man," lamented one of the women. She was a small woman with thread tied hair (*isi owu*) and dressed in a simple *Ankara* gown. She had a protruding stomach as a result of her pregnancy and that seemed to be the only big feature in her because she was a petite woman.

"*Chinasa* I suggest we keep quiet, and just walk quietly behind him. It is already so late, who knows what this man might do to us?" whispered her companion who was considerate enough to speak in hushed tones, unlike her friend. She was a fair woman with a more pleasant looking youthful appearance, unlike her friend who just sighed loudly.

"Nonsense," exclaimed Chinasa bravely. "We have nothing to fear *Ogechi*, my husband *Udenta* will see that we are safely returned home. He can take on this man any time." Ogechi remained quiet at the assurance of her friend deciding there was no use in talking again.

Their discussion ended immediately by the abrupt halt from the lunatic, Dalu. He turned towards them with his dark brown eyes glistening under the moonlight; at that very moment his appearance could be likened to the main antagonist in a horror play. They all held their breath in fear that he had heard all their gossips about him. The only man in the small group stepped timidly in front of the women and cleared his throat.

"Dalu let us pass," implored the man in a slightly unsteady voice.

Dalu tried but failed to stop the frown on his face, this only succeeded in making him more sinister than their imagination had painted him. "I do not wish to harm any of you," he explained ignoring their fear-stricken faces.

"Then get out of our way!" demanded Chinasa amidst the disapproving looks from her husband, and friend for her outburst.

Dalu having no choice sighed. "As you wish," he said moving away for them to proceed forward. They hurriedly walked past him seeing it as an opportunity to rid themselves of his unbearable presence. All too suddenly, they also halted in their footsteps finally seeing what Dalu had seen.

"It's a body!" shrieked the pregnant Chinasa as she gripped her husband's forearms in mortification.

"Is she dead?" asked Ogechi ignoring the rain that was wetting her hair as she moved closer to inspect the body lying on the floor. In front of them lay a girl dressed in a simple shirt and skirt. Although the darkness and the heavy rain showers obscured a full image of her, it was easy to make out her lithe frame lying seemingly lifeless on the muddy ground. It was hard to determine her age but from Dalu could see, she was young. In addition to that, the unhealthy look of her hollowed cheeks imitated the image of a person who was at the brink of death. The only sign that she could be alive was the movement of her fingers clutching a small bag desperately. After years of being the victim of unnecessary scrutiny, Dalu stood behind these people as a witness for the first time. He could see the tell-tale signs of judgement for a girl that most certainly needed their help.

"We will have to go and gather some youths, to at least bury her," suggested Udenta with obvious reluctance in his voice.

His wife followed suit, "this does not concern us, Ude. We should leave; she obviously is a bad omen." Her friend Ogechi nodded in agreement choosing to say nothing. "Let us go, we do not know the circumstances of her death," she continued.

From behind them, Dalu finally spoke unable to hide the irritation in his voice. "She is not dead." Anger bubbled within him, but he held it in check.

"How can you be sure?" demanded the prudish Udenta glaring at Dalu in disbelief.

He searched their faces slowly, and when he saw no value in explaining further to their closed off minds, he pushed past them and bent towards the girl. He placed his palm above her nose and felt her exhale faint air.

"While you all believe that she is dead, she breathes," he revealed in a cold voice that conveyed his disappointment and distaste for their judgemental behaviour towards this helpless girl. Without so little as a glance towards them, he searched the girl cautiously until he found the sign he was looking for; two puncture holes on her left ankle. Carefully, he pressed two fingers around the wound and held it tightly as he ripped the lower piece of his shirt which he tied securely around the spot. He shocked the other people with him when he lifted the girl easily into his arms and continued on his way. He had no intentions of arguing further when a life was at stake.

*

In her dream, she was a bird with the freedom to take flight anywhere she so pleased. She took the shape of a dove receiving kisses from the golden rays of the warm sun. The earth welcomed her in acceptance and

13

an offering of peacefulness so gentle that she began floating in the clouds without her wings flapping. Her peace was interrupted by a darkness so thick that it blinded her. Her instincts immediately kicked in, insisting on the need to escape from such peril. Instead of the dove she was, she transformed back to her human form and ran as fast as she could because she was engulfed in the fear of what may happen to her if she stopped. Suddenly pursuers all equipped with torches and machetes chased after her, screaming angrily at her. It was clear that their intention was to kill her who was their common enemy. Without a clue of where the sudden strength in her limbs emerged from, she ran with all she had because it was apparent that this was a race for her life. No matter how much they called her name "*Simdi*," she did not dare stop.

The will to live which was suddenly ignited within her came as a surprise because in the past she had given up on the value of her life, calling for death's consumption of her being. Why was she suddenly overcome with the zeal to live? It was until she continued running ceaselessly that a realisation came to her mind; she had no idea where she was running to. Her pursuers caught up to her circling her like the prey that they had forced her to become. Faced with imminent danger, her instincts kicked in and she screamed so loud in a desperate attempt to channel out all the frustration, anger, and fear she felt from her present situation.

Abruptly, she came back into reality as she forcefully sat up from her slumber. She took in her surroundings from the middle of the worn bed she lay in. The room was made of dark grey cement walls and a crusty smell she assumed was from dust that gathered on the walls and in the corners of the window. A feeling of emptiness engulfed her as she looked around the room that was almost devoid of furniture except the bed she was sitting on and the small stool beside her. When she inhaled the air, it was stale with dust particles on her teeth. This prompted her to cough but luckily as she turned, she saw a cup of water placed beside her on the short stool. With shaky dirty fingers, she lifted the metal cup and drank greedily, some of the clear liquid seeping down the sides of her mouth and down her throat.

The door which was just a straw curtain that served the purpose of casting an illusion of privacy into the room rose up, and Simdi found herself holding her breath in anticipation of seeing the face of her saviour. From the shadows emerged the tall bulky figure of a man with hair worn in long dreadlocks. This was the first time she was seeing anyone with such hair, but the dirtiness of the locks made them unpleasant to even admire. It hung loosely down to his shoulders while a scruffy beard covered half of his face. To be honest, it was hard to look past the dirty and unkempt appearance of the man, but she tried her best not to stare. Looking upwards, she averted her gaze and inwardly cringed, trying not to squirm under his cautious dark eyes that observed her coldly.

"My bag?" It was the first thing that she actually said to him in her state of uneasiness. Her conscience was quick to call her an ingrate for words that were not in any way appreciative towards the man, but she ignored the taunting voice. The man pointed behind her where the small worn bag hung.

"Where am I ...?" she asked trying to steady her voice. The man averted his eyes, before answering her. "Umi."

She frowned confusedly because she had never heard of such a place all her life, "*Imo*?" she pressed on. He shook his head, "far from there."

Her eyes shot up as the severity of her circumstances finally dawned on her. She could not remain here because she could not afford to be caught. "I can't stay here ...," she told him in a hoarse voice as she attempted to stand up, but a sharp pain stopped her. "Ahhhh!" she screamed tumbling back on the bed.

The man stood unfazed at her discomfort, "maybe after your leg heals then you can go wherever you deem suitable, but for now you can barely move." He did not wait for her to reply before he turned to leave.

With his disappearing back, Simdi raised her left leg inspecting the damage for the first time. It was covered in bandages, with some type of herbal scent emitting from it. She placed it back where it lay on the foot of the bed frowning. Who was this man? What was his motive for saving her? Was she safe staying here? Even when the man re-entered the room a second time; these thoughts surrounded her, and she found herself watching him suspiciously.

He set the food down for her and at closer inspection, she discovered that it was a bowl of yam porridge. He left her to her food only to return with a fresh cup of water. "Eat to be stronger," he stated vaguely as he finally exited the room for good.

Once he left, Simdi contemplated if she should trust this stranger enough to eat the food that he offered her. To be honest she was very hungry especially since she had gone days without eating. The months that she had spent fleeing; she had gone without much substantial food, relying on only fruits, water and, on lucky occasions, bread. Her saviour though unlikely, did not seem like a bad person. After all, he had tended to her wound and allowed her to recuperate in his home, even though she was also a stranger to him. There was no reason why he could not have left her to die on the road but instead, he saved her.

For the first time in a long while, Simdi decided to give another human being the benefit of the doubt. In one deciding moment, she picked up the bowl of porridge and put the first spoon into her mouth as an indication of her decision to abandon her fear and utilize the opportunity handed over to her. The food was surprisingly edible, and she devoured it savouring the oily mixture of the porridge and the yam. Temporarily, she would forget the past that was never far too behind her.

*

A chunk of dry wood sat on the table in front of him as he gripped his chisel. Dalu stood studying it briefly; he was a sculptor who took pleasure in giving life to something as lifeless as wood. There was always this intriguing quality about looking at plain wood before he gave it meaning. He had control over unmasking the hidden character behind the shapeless object. Tonight, as he continued to scrape the wood, he decided that he would make the sculpture a fox. With that in mind, he picked up his chisel and set to work. Although his sculptures were never appreciated in Umi as a result of the villagers' refusal to patronize him, he was somewhat a known sculptor outside Umi. Day after day he made his money by leaving Umi to other villages where he sold his creations. People were intrigued by the elegant lines of his sculptures and the careful intricate carvings that seemed to promise them a story. He was careful at what he did, and some people could even say that he was a perfectionist when it came to his work because none of his sculptures were disfigured, unless on the rare occasion when he intentionally chose to disfigure them.

The working silence in his workshop was disrupted by shuffling sounds coming from the girl in the room behind his workshop. She must have finished her food, but he remained where he was seated unable to face her. It was not that he disliked her after all, he had saved her life. The truth was that he was avoiding the awkwardness that seemed to surround their encounters. He opted to avoid human interaction as much as he could due to the emotional scar that the betrayals of the village people had left within him. Waking up to the stench of his dead sons was enough to change his life forever. He would never understand why they hated him so much. What was so wrong about him that they had spit curses on him rather than come to his aid? These questions constantly haunted him, and he never had answers for them. To protect himself from the village and its treachery he had hidden far away in his home seeking only to leave it when he could not avoid it. The memories of that day never really returned fully to him, but he knew the basics. He still remembered that it had been a few days after the untimely death of his wife and their unborn child. Overcome by exhaustion from silently grieving, he had fallen asleep only to be woken up by the cries of one of his sons. When he rushed outside, they were both lying unconscious. In his state of panic, he had raced to the village seeking help from the healer who often consulted there, but his efforts had been in vain because they still died.

The fragility of the situation that the girl had been in when he found her was what inspired him to help her. Just like him, the people had been quick to label her a '*bad omen*.' Something inside him snapped when they all stood there already judging her, forgetting that the girl was on the brink of dying. His weariness towards life and also his cowardice to take it, was the reason he chose to be a recluse. Saving her was a decision that he made on impulse; he had allowed the human side of him which still felt sympathy override his need to shield himself from the cruelty of human nature. In a rare moment, even when he should have upheld his image of lunacy, he had broken that stereotype by showing compassion that the 'sane' people could not show. Her presence was something new to him, and until he understood what it meant, he diligently continued his work, opting to ignore the sounds he heard and rather focused on the intricate carvings he branded his sculpture with.

2

Moisture ....

*T*he dog barked, and Dalu woke up. He rarely slept at night but after six hours of carving, his muscles and limbs had gone soft. He had succumbed to the lure of sleep in his chair; the slumber welcomed for the first time in a while. Looking around, he heard thrashing sounds from the room that the girl slept in. Everything in him wanted to ignore her as he had done previously, but he knew more than anyone else what a nightmare sounded like.

He walked briskly towards her room lifting up the curtain. She lay there at the centre of the room, her body drenched in sweat, even though the room was so cold. Being a man who had struggled so much with unwanted nightmares, he recognized immediately that she was fighting an internal battle. It was evident in the way her toes curled up and her fingers clenched in the fear that the nightmare brought with it. Without a moment's hesitation, he left her only for a moment to resurface with a small bowl of lukewarm water and a small towel. Bending beside her, he soaked the towel into the water before placing it on her forehead and cleaning the sweat beads off it. This close to her, his first impression of her was that she was neither beautiful nor ugly; she looked too unhealthy to even be considered passable. He must have made a sound loud enough for her to regain consciousness because the next thing he knew, she abruptly opened her eyes in shock. Dalu quickly moved away from her as he took his spot next to the window while she gradually adjusted to the darkness around the room. He heard her clear her throat, fighting within herself not to appear weak; but she did a poor job at it. He could tell by merely looking at her that she was as frightened from the nightmare as any normal person should be.

"Thank... you," she said in a cracked voice.

He did not know how to react to it, so he shifted uncomfortably. Dalu was used to scorn, hate, disgust, and even malice, but he had never received gratitude. This was a foreign feeling for him and hearing her thank him so easily almost made him question if he had entered an alternate reality or the afterlife. He never thought he would hear such words from anyone.

His surprise at her gratitude ushered in the presence of a thick silence which was eventually broken when the girl cleared her throat again as if demanding for his attention.

"What happened to my leg?" she asked trying to sit up, and at the same time remove the towel that had been placed on her forehead.

"You were bitten by a snake. I stopped the venom from spreading further, but if we must acknowledge divine intervention, I would say that you were lucky I found you when I did," he replied as he slowly moved towards her to collect the towel. There was nothing else he could attribute to that day other than pure luck. Not everyone could still remain alive once the venom of a snake had entered their body, but this girl had managed to stay alive for God knows how long.

"Luck you say....?" There was disbelief in her voice. It seemed as if she was not shocked that she had survived a snake bite; instead, she was in awe that he believed she was lucky. Her face turned serious again, "Why did you...help me?" she asked swallowing nervously. He saw her hesitate briefly, but then courageously continued. "You helped me even though you do not know me...why?" This time her voice was firmer.

Again, another silence stretched between them. Dalu shrugged replaying countless reasons why he could have left her and in their midst emerged a singular purpose of rescuing her. "You reminded me of myself some time ago when I woke up to the rain on my skin, pain behind my head, and not a single person close by to help me." He saw the disbelief on her face that he had answered her. She looked as though she wanted to say something else, but she was interrupted by the insistent barking of the dog outside. He left his corner by the window, and instead, collected the bowl before attempting to leave the room.

In a rare moment of thoughtfulness, he turned towards her again offering an explanation, "My dog is hungry." When she did not reply he took that as a green light and left the room quietly.

When Dalu was outside, he looked down gratefully at his dog for saving him from another awkward encounter with the girl. As he set the bowl of leftovers for the dog and long-time companion, he questioned what exactly he would do with the girl inside. It was obvious that something was chasing her and sooner or later; it would find her. It would not be wise if he was caught between her and the *what*.

*

He was a little boy, with adoring eyes that observed his father crushing different herbal leaves together. His father was a hard worker with sun-darkened skin brought about by his daily visits to the herb fields; he was blessed with a bulky build and several trophy scars on his back which he wore proudly. Each scar whether jagged or faint, had a very interesting story to it that his father promised he would one day tell him of when he was older.

As an adventurous young boy, Dalu never missed the chance of exploring the herb fields with his father. He was always thrilled to watch the expert way his father identified each plant one after the other and picking the ones that could save lives from the discarded ones that would take those same lives.

"Dalu pay attention!" scolded his father when he noticed that Dalu's eyes strayed to the line of ants beside him. When his attention returned, his father continued. "Plants, like us are alive. Even though they have no mouth to talk; it is their decision whether to save our lives or to take it away from us."

He gave his father a toothy grin even though almost all his front teeth had fallen off. "They are just plants at our mercy Papa, how can you say that they make such decisions?" he asked his father with the childish interest of a seven-year-old boy.

"Dalu, just because you seem bigger than other living things does not mean that they are at your mercy," chastised his father before continuing. "For one, you do not pull it as though it were a weed. It is coaxed into freedom; the roots carefully dusted to remove most of the sand particles. When it is cooked, it should be boiled to tenderness while extracting the juices that it holds. If crushed and pounded without patience or with the arrogance of knowledge it becomes a poison son."

Dalu nodded intrigued with the way his father's dark face seemed to light up as he explained everything with a knowing expression.

Scratching his tangled short hair, he asked. "Will I ever be like you father? As good as you are with plants?"

To that question his father chuckled, his voice echoing through the small cave they had gone into for herb scouting. "You'll be better, you have to believe that." The smile on his father's face had so much faith and belief in it that Dalu could not help but accept that he would be able to do all that his father envisioned he could.

*

He woke up abruptly, a bead of sweat adorning his forehead. How long had it been since he had dreamt of his late father? The emotions the dream evoked within him was a prison that he had tried so hard to escape. He had fought continuously to forget how good his life had been a long time ago, yet the cruel thoughts refused to leave him.

"Leave me ALONE!" he agonized in a loud pained voice as angry unwanted tears spilled down his cheeks.

He missed them all; his parents, his wife and his children. Why could he not rid himself of these painful memories? When would he finally find peace in this loneliness that they had all left him in? Breathing unevenly, he insistently beat his head on the floor, craving the darkness and silence that came with unconsciousness. Eventually, he passed out on the floor, blood coating his forehead.

*

Simdi woke up abruptly to angry screams reverberating throughout the whole house. The screams changed from frustrated shrieks to pained wails, which sent cautious fear throughout her whole body. How could someone feel this much anguish?

She wondered how long he had lived in such a way. This man who had saved her; who was he? While he looked like a lunatic, her brief interactions with him and his mannerism proved that he was not insane. He was a person who understood what it meant to hide. Unlike the other people she met, this man did not pry into her life. She could tell that he was curious about who she was, but he had not insisted on her sharing her story. They were both strangers pushed together by circumstances, but this aloofness prompted the insistent need in her to gain more closure about him; anything at all that would make her understand this mystery surrounding him. Following his screams, she questioned her judgment in remaining here. She knew from bitter experiences that it was better to never prolong the duration of time she spent at one place. The past had taught her in harrowing ways, never to get attached to the people who she came across because she never stayed long enough. However, for some unexplainable reason, she did not want to leave here even after her leg would have gotten better. There was a possibility that she could rest longer here, especially since it was far from the River village. She waited for several minutes and surely soon enough; the thud sounds from the man's room faded. Against her better judgment she worried about him.

Closing her eyes, she forced herself to forget about the sounds she had heard earlier. Minding her own business was a bitter lesson that life had taught her.

*

Sunlight

The rays of sunlight seeped into his room, caressing his cheeks with the warmth they carried. Slowly he opened his eyes and the first thing that registered to him was the pain concentrated on his forehead. It felt like his head was going to fall off at any moment. He saw the dried blood on the floor beside his bed and the flies that were beginning to gather around it. He struggled and failed to stand up without wobbling. A wave of dizziness washed over him, and he desperately held on to the wooden stool beside him. "Be calm," he whispered to himself trying to get steady breathing.

He closed his eyes exhaling harshly, as his nostrils flared open. When he calmed down, he let go of the stool choosing to ignore the pain that came with his swollen forehead. Inside his washroom, he found a weakened rag that he tore from one of his disregarded clothes and set out to wash the wound using simple antiseptic herbs. He wrapped the cloth around his stinging head and spat out saliva that formed in his mouth. A sense of amusement overtook him as he left the washroom which was just an ill-used term for a room that he barely used. When was the last time he showered? Days, weeks, or maybe a month; who knew? If he smelt bad, no one said anything about it. Although to be frank, people never got too close to him in the first place. He was sure that if the girl was displeased with him, she would have voiced out her opinion. Out of consideration towards her, he decided to remove his week-old worn shirt and replaced it with another one with a tear on the sleeves and hem.

*

His cooking this time was done carelessly, the potatoes were burnt so bad that it almost looked charred. The stew was even worse altogether; it was too salty to be considered tasty. The pain in his skull made him feel less guilty as he served it to her without a second thought. Until he could think clearly, she would make do with whatever he gave her. On entering her room, he could now see her clearly thanks to the soft light cast by the sun. She looked better this morning; he could say that she appeared to be more alive than last night when she had been so pale and the eye bags under her eyes, hollow. Today she seemed to have gotten a little rest, but her cheeks were still not as filled out as it should be. Her lips had even managed to recover some colour on it, leaving it with a pale pink appearance, rather than the odd greyish tone it had the day before. No wonder people mistook her for dead.

Somewhere at the back of his mind, he wondered if she had heard him shouting last night. It would explain why she was yet to speak to him. In the daylight, he could make out her face well enough to tell that she was a young woman in her early twenties. Her hair although short, was very curly with some parts uneven as if she had held the strands in one hand and cut it with a jagged-edged instrument. She was lean, and he blamed that on malnutrition. He was sure that if she was well fed, she would have a slender healthy figure. Her skin was a bronzed caramel colour, brought about by many days of walking under the hot sun; in fact, she was thoroughly tanned from the sun. She had a small nose, and underneath it were full heart shaped lips. She wore no earrings, but there were holes in her ears that indicated that she had worn one at some point in her life. Last night he had concluded that she was neither beautiful nor ugly but standing in front of her with the light giving him a clear vision of her; he was blown away by her eyes. It was a captivating rare colour that he had only seen from a few chanced encounters with foreigners but even then, he had never seen it up close to feel their impact. Her eyes were a hazel mix of light brown with specks of gold. It made him wonder about her parentage; was she a foreigner? How could one person be blessed with such beautiful eyes? He wanted to ask her this, but instead, he kept quiet knowing from experience that she would close off if he asked the wrong question. She was too protective of herself.

As he bent down to place the plate he held, he saw her observing his forehead. If she had any questions, she must have decided not to ask them. He left her side going to stand by the window again; he had no idea what to say to her at that point so instead, he watched her face in silent observation. He tried not to smirk mischievously at how her face scrunched in distaste at the bittersweet taste of the burnt potatoes and salty stew. The fact that he derived a little delight in her discomfort spoke volumes of his deteriorating knowledge of how he was expected to treat other human beings, especially young women. He wanted to laugh or even smile in amusement, as though his poor cooking was an inside joke, but he decided against it. How long had it been since he had felt the impulse to laugh or smile? He doubted that he would recognize his own voice or the expression on his face if he even tried to do either. He heard her tap the plate to get his occupied attention.

"I have a favour to ask you," she started saying while he remained unmoving waiting for her to make her request.

"Already you have done so much for me but… I am afraid that I stink. Is it possible that I can take a bath as soon as possible?" she asked uncomfortably, her face fighting not to look embarrassed.

It suddenly felt too much to hold it in and he burst out laughing. He must have seemed weirder than he already was, but her sudden formality while asking about something as simple as a bath seemed amusing.

"I am sorry, but you looked like you sucked on the sourest lime on earth just now." He stopped laughing and observed her. He should have known that she would need to freshen up. Not everyone was as nonchalant as he was when it came to personal hygiene; it was not as though he had anyone to impress.

"I have a washroom which is not too far from here," he revealed before leaving the room briefly.

It took about five minutes to boil the hot water for her to bathe with. He left her some soap to use, wondering if it was still usable since it had been there for a long time. It was in the process of returning to her room to fetch her that he realized he was beginning to associate what was his, like hers. It was not *her* room but a spare room that he put her in. Nothing except the bag that she came in with, belonged to her. She would leave one day and what he considered hers would naturally continue to be his.

When he returned, she was seated on the bed clutching her bag and looking at him expectantly. He wondered how she had moved from the bed to where her bag hung. He came to her holding a makeshift crutch that he had made for her the first night when he rescued her. It was in that moment of creativity that he acquired the empathy to consider how uncomfortable she would be whenever she limped without any form of support unless he decided to carry her, which he was sure would repulse her. There was surprise in her eyes when she saw the crutch, and this gave him an unexplainable satisfaction, which he hid with indifference.

"It will make walking easier but if you do not want it, you are free to reject it." He knew he was bluffing, he wanted her to accept it.

She accepted it without hesitation and briefly inspected it for a while before looking up at him with a smile that made him momentarily motionless. For a man who rarely smiled, seeing it worn so beautifully by another human being left him totally unprepared for his dumbfounded reaction. He was beginning to fear what she would look like once she recovered from her obvious malnutrition and the effects of the fading poison.

"No, I appreciate it ...thank you," she told him softly. "Please help me up?" she asked politely when he just stood there so out of his element.

He nodded, still so alien at receiving gratitude. When he bent closer to her than he usually did, he saw her flinch with her nostrils flaring open involuntarily to perceive his stench thanks to months of not bothering to wash properly. She did not talk as he steadied her, but she looked away and he guessed she was trying to block it by holding her breath. In that room, standing next to this girl; Dalu who had never cared about what anyone thought of him was instantly hit by a wave of self-consciousness.

When they were finally inside his room, he moved away from her and said, "I will leave you to yourself. I am not too far in case you are done and need help returning." Without waiting for her reply, he turned and left her before she passed out from trying so hard not to breathe next to him.

*

Simdi sighed as the warm water washed over her. It was so comforting that she closed her eyes relishing the feel of the water running down her naked skin. She was sitting on the stool, her injured leg raised away from where the water could touch it. She washed her hair using her nails to scrub off the dirt which gathered from all the sand, and mud she had encountered. Opening her eyes, she looked around the washroom, noticing all the cobwebs and dust surrounding it. It was obvious that her saviour, who was yet to tell her his name, did not make use of this place. The man reeked, but she did not feel that it was her duty to point that out to him. She would be blind if she did not notice the torn cloth that had been wrapped around his swollen forehead. It had not been there last night because although the room had been slightly dark, she had been able to see a little of his uninjured face. She sighed drying herself with a small hand towel she had taken with her from the last place she left behind. The dress she picked from her small bag was a worn simple floral gown, that was given to her by her *nne*. Thoughts of her mother caused tears to gather in the corners of her eyes, but she held it in because this was the last thing she needed to display in front of the man. It was a vow deep within that she would not shed tears anymore because her mother would not want her to dwell in the tragedy that had befallen them.

After she dressed, she came out of the washroom quietly, but she did not call for the man. She had no ill intentions, but she could not fight her curiosity about the man. She wanted to know more about him, and it was what led her to look around his room. For a man like him, his room was a stark contrast to him. While it was dusty, it did not hide the emphasis placed on arrangement. The wide bed was pushed away from the window to the farthest corner away from sunlight, the small stool was aligned vertically from the bed frame. There was no wardrobe, but even his dirty clothes were piled neatly beside the bathroom door. It did not make sense because the man himself was a mess, she had assumed that when she walked into this room it would be in disarray, but her assumption was wrong. The only thing that seemed out of place was the dried blood stains beside the bed. She stood still, transfixed by the small stain that had flies hovering around it on the floor. It made her question why this man would inflict himself with such pain? She was so deep in thought that she did not hear when he walked into the room. It took all her willpower not to look guilty that he caught her intrusively observing his room. She fixed him with a bored expression which he returned with narrowed untrusting eyes.

"You did not call me." It was not a question; he was accusing her.

Her eyes acting on mere instinct focused on his bandaged forehead, "why would you harm yourself this way?" she blurted out without even considering his reaction.

He stiffened where he stood, holding his breath as his face hardened in an angry scowl. When he finally spoke, his voice was resigned. "It is nothing for you to be concerned with," he replied brushing aside her concern. "If you are done, then we can head back out."

Simdi flinched because ever since she had woken up here, this was the first time he was sounding this way to her. In other instances, he had at least maintained his politeness towards her but right now he was putting her, in her place. Salvaging what was left of her dignity, she shrugged telling herself she had no reason to feel hurt by how he brushed her off. He was right; she was encroaching on what did not concern her. She walked past him ignoring the pain her leg sent out through her whole body as another wave of silence and tension filled the room.

She would have disregarded it, but her pride pushed her to act as she turned back to him and demanded in frustration. "What have I done wrong? Why are you so annoyed?" she demanded, shocked at how wounded she sounded. Something at the back of her mind kept nagging her that if this tension was not resolved, things would never be alright for as long as she decided to remain here.

While his face was expressionless, his words hit the nail right at the centre. "You stood there in the centre of this room, and you judged me." When she could not reply, he simply ushered her out of his room.

Simdi sat slowly on the stool near the window and stared outside making a mental note to curb her curiosity about him. He was wrong when he concluded that she judged him when all she had really done was assume that he would conform to the image he presented outwardly. If she could correct his accusation, she would make sure she made it clear that she never judged him. She was in no position to judge anyone. In this new place that she found herself in; this nameless man was probably the only ally that she had. It would be a wrong move to make him a foe.

*

The sunny atmosphere that afternoon did nothing to stop the chilliness left by the rain from the previous night. Dalu was inside his small farm planting corn seeds while he did his best to ignore the harsh sun beating down his bare back. He was grateful to Mother Nature for shedding rainy tears on the ground because it was easy to make soil moulds for his crops. Today he worked harder than usual; the sweat dripping down his back, and bandaged head. It stung so much that he kept scolding himself for being so stupid; he had acted too rashly.

It was different having someone else inside his house. It was beginning to dawn on him that her continued presence in his home would infringe heavily on his comfort zone. Now that the haze of his anger was gone, Dalu realised that his reaction had been blown out of proportion. Undeniably, he would admit that it was unsettling when he had caught her standing there in the middle of his room with her very expressive face conveying what she had thought of him. It annoyed him greatly that she of all people judged him. He did not owe anyone any explanation, which was why he had chosen to live far away from the people in his village. He chose to live this life only caring about the basic things in life such as filling his stomach with food and sheltering his worn self. Living a reclusive life had been an unconscious decision made without fully comprehending that it would grow on him over time. He discovered that his imposed ignorance of all the many pleasures offered by life secured a small semblance of the peace he once had before those six years.

He was brought out of his reverie by the cheerful sounds of children laughing. He swallowed apprehensively as his eyes followed the concentration of the sun rays to a familiar spot around the mango tree in front of his house. He stood there motionlessly staring with his mouth wide open, at the glistening sunshine rays that cascaded the mango tree like precious crystals. The image of two little boys materialized in front of him like a long-awaited stage play being unveiled. They engaged in a simple game of sticks and stones and upon seeing him, they both gave him bright smiles that broke his aching heart.

"Papa *bia fu*...... come and see what *Ifeanyi* showed me," beckoned the boys pointing at the shapes they had created with the sticks.

He walked towards them with shaky legs, his throat suddenly too tight. It was not real; he knew that they were no longer real because after so long of reliving this torment, he could now tell reality apart from fantasy. The life he lived was plagued with the cruel gift of remembrance that never allowed him to forget. He had indulged in alcohol at the early stages of his grief, to the point that it stopped affecting him. Giving into his wistful thinking, he walked to the tree and sat beside them admiring what had once been his; two healthy boys with similar brown skin like his, although theirs were slightly lighter due to his wife's contribution in their birth. They bore his dark eyes with their limbs and teeth all strong. They had been four and five years respectively at the time of their untimely deaths. Although his wife had fought against teaching them a language foreign to their traditional Igbo dialect, Dalu had taught his sons English as his late father had done for him. In his eyes, these children would go places and he wanted to prepare them for that. Perhaps his ambition for his children had been too much; it must have been the reason why fate had callously gambled with him.

His oldest son *Oyirinnaya,* whom he fondly called *Oyiri* turned his smiling face towards his father to display the beautiful gapped tooth that he inherited from his mother. Dalu knew what would happen if he attempted to speak to them even if it was just a simple "*my sons,*" but he still tried. Just as he predicted, as soon as he uttered those words, they faded leaving specks of dust as his only proof of their visit. He felt his energy vanish from him as he slumped on the tree, angry tears falling down his cheeks. He needed a lot of things in his life, but what he did not need was the binding memories of his past that haunted him. He lay unmoving, ignoring the ants that climbed on his body, for a split second he wished desperately for the ground to open and swallow him. He wanted to join them, but he was too cowardly to end his life. Each time he tried, memories of the vow that he made to his wife about living on chastised him. Not in a million years could he have predicted that he would end up like this; a mess of a man who constantly begged death to take pity on him and end his misery.

*

One of Simdi's best memories was of a woman uniquely different from the rest of the people in her hometown. She was a beautiful shy woman with neatly weaved hair, clad in some of the prettiest gowns Simdi had ever seen. She had a round smiling face that evoked happiness within everyone around her. She was a pinnacle of kindness and reliance which most people in the village called upon in their time of assistance. She was teacher; a brilliant one that was admired by the young girls and men in the village. They were taken by her floral gowns and easy sophistication which were rare inside their small village. She was their role model and a figure of knowledge who trained the younger ones to be better people for the future. This amazing woman was everything to Simdi.

They lived inside a quaint teacher's home. Although it might have been small, it was comfortable with its consistent fragrance of subtle lilac, and the aromatic scent of already eaten breakfast. It was enough for them because above everything else, their little home was a place filled with warmth and love.

"Simdi...." came her mother's calm voice on that particular day. Simdi looked up at her smiling freely, "yes *nne*?"

Her mother grinned fondly at her and ruffled her hair. Although they were not connected by blood or birth, Simdi loved her nonetheless because she was the only person in the world she knew as her mother. The story of her parentage and how they came to be together as a two-unit family was still a mystery. Simdi should have been curious about it, but she had long since concluded that what truly mattered was that she had her mother with her.

"What does the sky show you?" asked her mother who pointed upwards. This was a simple philosophical game they played each time they were free. Simdi hummed contemplatively as she considered her mother's question.

"Would it be distressing if I said *too much?*" she questioned as a small frown formed on her face.

Her mother shook her head in encouragement patting her head. "No, my daughter.... nothing is too much for you to see."

Again, she studied the blue canvas with curious eyes. "I dream of the sky mum, of floating and riding the soft white clouds. I see shapes at night, and I see the beautiful bright stars." She stopped mid-speech as she contemplated whether to continue. "The truth *nne* is that sometimes in my dreams the sky is absent, and in its wake are visions of a time when I must leave you. Why do I see these things mum? Why would I leave you?" Even as she spoke, she felt a thick feeling of apprehension overtaking her. This was no longer a light game of guessing instead, it was now a conversation tainted with a sense of heavy foreboding.

Almost on instinct, she pulled a fake happy smile in a bid to reassure her mother, but the woman saw right through her. Simdi found herself engulfed in a comforting hug that ended with her witnessing her mother's happy façade crumbling for the first time. It felt like her mother was finally offloading the baggage that she had held onto for too long, and Simdi allowed her to weep. She too felt tears running down her cheeks for a burden she was unaware that she carried.

"Look at us, crying in fear of the unknown," muttered Simdi wiping her eyes.

Her mother chuckled humourlessly and looked up to the sky, "fear keeps you alive Simdi. If there is ever a time when you must run, do it bearing in mind that I will always be with you. You may leave home, but I will never leave you. I will always be in here," she vowed touching where her heartbeat silently in hidden worry. Would there ever be a time when they would not be together?

3

Change....

*D*alu had no recollection of how long he stayed under the mango tree but when he opened his eyes, the stormy evening clouds welcomed him. Disappointment washed over him when he realised that he had fallen asleep under the tree with the work he had started in the farm, unfinished. He shivered wondering if it would also rain tonight; he wished it did not because he needed his wood dry for carving. Standing slowly, he stretched and decided to conclude his farming at another time; he chose instead to prepare the meal for that evening. Bearing in mind that the breakfast he served to the girl had been a colossal disappointment, he began cooking with great care this time. As a principle he was never one for leftover food, so he measured the ingredients to ascertain the right quantity that would feed all three of them. He was pleased with himself that the beans porridge did not burn this time, neither was the food too salty. Going back to his behaviour this morning, he wanted to appease his guest because she was not the cause of his problems. He needed to stop comparing her to the inhabitants of Umi. He wanted her to feel safe around him, but at the same time, they needed to establish the boundaries of their individual privacy. This meal would be his peace offering to her.

The minute Dalu lifted the curtain to her room, he immediately sensed that the girl was not alright. She turned her face from him as she sat quietly in the corner away from the bed. Even when he placed the food beside her, she did not even give the food a glance as she shook her head in refusal. He frowned, a little annoyed because she had easily rejected something that he had gone through a lot of effort to prepare in the hopes of extending an olive branch to her.

"What is the matter?" he bit out, his voice sounding sharper than he had intended.

"I'm not hungry," she whispered shakily.

"Look...girl, you must be hungry. You need food to get stronger and heal," attempted Dalu again. He also tried his best to refrain from scoffing.

It must have been something he said because she turned sharply at him. "I am not a girl; you are not allowed to belittle me or my maturity. I am a woman and I have a name! I have a name!" she declared almost shouting.

Dalu moved away from her as he pleaded with himself to calm down. She was clearly venting her frustrations at him. If he was in the mood to vent too; he would have pointed out that her leanness and near state of starvation made her look nothing like a woman, but he would be the bigger person just this once.

"Ok what is it then? What is this name that you need me to identify you by?" he asked pinching the rib of his nose impatiently.

She hmphed and then she glared at him. "Simdi...Chisimdi Ejim but...it's always been Simdi," she explained as if it should matter to him.

He knew he should have left her at that juncture, but he decided to be thoughtful and ask, "are you alright Simdi? You seem more weighed down than your usual self." Even in his own ears, he knew that the statement would infuriate her further.

She scoffed loudly and eyed him in displeasure, "normally when someone offers their name, the polite thing to do is reciprocate and not insult them."

Dalu almost walked over to the nearest wall to bang his head. "Dalu," he bit out and scratched his head, "why are you so difficult? You always make things harder than it is supposed to be. First, it was a bath that you had such a hard time asking, and now for my name you want to scratch out my eyes..."

He stopped talking when she limped in front of him and looked straight at him challengingly, "so I am difficult!!! If I am that much of a hardship, why did you not just leave me out there to die? Who forced you to save me? Who?" she shouted pointing her small slender index finger at his chest.

She was too close, too much in his personal bubble and without thinking he lashed out as well. He gripped the finger that was pointed at him and admitted vehemently, "oh believe me I am starting to regret it." Right before his very eyes, Simdi crumbled. He watched as the fire in her eyes died out and it was then he noticed the puffiness in them. She must have been crying before he entered the room. He could not speak because he was lost for words, but he released her finger and left the room without saying anything to her.

Had it always been this hard interacting with another person?

Venturing into Umi was reserved for dire situations. The place of his birth was a very small community where people regularly gossiped about everything. Dalu continued walking and did his best to ignore the stares that he received; he was certain that stories of him picking up a girl must have spread throughout the village. He paid no attention to them until he reached his destination; the central market where almost every trader sold their goods. Little children ran around the open space, some dirty with mucus running down their noses, and others relatively cleaner with sand in their hair. The careless abandonment with which they chased after one another made him pause to observe them fondly. For the remainder of their childhood, they would not be burdened with the worries that consumed adults. He knew that one day these children would eventually become like the adults of the village who were an embodiment of scorn and hate which characterized the villagers. In the depth of his heart, he hoped that they would find their own path rather than emulate the judgmental people that flocked round every nook and cranny of Umi.

The next few seconds were a blur to him; he registered a sharp pain spreading across his back, and then almost like time moved in slow motion, he saw himself tumbling to the ground. People gathered around him, but none of them attempted to help him. As he struggled to stand, he realised that he had fallen into cow faeces. The stench was unbearable, and it took him all his restraint not to throw up. Even for him, this was the height of his disregard for hygiene. He came face to face with his assailant; a young boy no older than sixteen years with a cart, who looked at him unapologetically while flashing the pole he used in assaulting him.

"What are you looking at mad man...*oye ara,*" the boy asked in a condescending voice as he brazenly taunted Dalu.

Dalu burst out laughing bitterly, "you a mere child who has no understanding behind the origin of this hatred towards me has joined the bandwagon... I hope you will stand this confident when Fate finds you." It was not funny the way he was treated, it was painful and degrading.

He stopped laughing as he saw the satisfaction in the eyes of the people who gathered to witness his disgrace in the hands of this boy. He tried but failed to ignore the pang of hurt his heart felt, it was not the first time he was being openly shunned; he should have been accustomed to it, but it only succeeded in reminding him of how alone he truly was in this world. After all, he was the orphaned child of a woman the people hated with as much venom as they did him. The only relatives from his father's lineage had long since distanced themselves from him.

An angry voice suddenly broke through the entertained spectators. "Have you people no shame? You saw this miscreant insulting a man twice his age, and you all just stood watching?" Dalu instantly recognized the voice which could only belong to one person; *Nwakaego*. She was his late mother's friend and the only person that ever really stood up for him against the villagers. The people began to disperse, but the gossips stood to see how this would end.

Without hesitation, she charged at the boy and slapped him so hard across the face that he was thrown to the ground. "Apologize!" she demanded standing tall and glorious in her grey hair, and authoritative eyes.

It was only a fool that would dare challenge her because she was the president of Umi market union. She was also a woman that many people considered an opinion leader, no one needed to be on her bad side in Umi. The boy looked conflicted at her order; on one hand he felt smug at having disgraced Dalu, but on the other hand, he did not want to incur the wrath of the popular Nwakaego. She was a woman who even men feared; her influence was known everywhere in Umi.

"Sorry mad man," he spat out grudgingly still holding his stinging cheeks.

Nwakaego raised her hand again ready to beat him but Dalu decided to put an end to this whole incident.

"I do not need his apology," he stated giving the boy one of his most distasteful looks before turning around and continuing towards his destination. Behind him, Nwakaego followed in silence.

He stopped in front of Nwakaego's shop and she beckoned on him to enter ignoring the disapproving looks she received from her patrons. The shop had undergone a lot of expansion over the years, it did not feel as small as it once had. When he was younger, he remembered his parents telling him that the woman sold almost all kinds of foodstuff in Umi. She had an assortment of rice, beans, tubers of yam, cocoyam, plantain, potato, '*abacha*', '*ukwa*', '*akidi*,' with different provisions and condiments. Her shop was one of the largest, and frequently visited in Umi because no other shop could compete with her when it came to the quality and freshness of her goods. Nwakaego was part of his past before he had become the "mad man." There had been a time when he was an entirely different man. As a boy, he had enjoyed the wind in his hair, especially the thrill he felt each time he rode his bicycle down the market path. Umi once accepted him. Although it had not been fully, at least they had not thrown things at him or made a mockery of who he was. In return, he had tried to fit in even if it was hard to do when no one allowed him to forget his mother's lineage. Inside this shop brought back memories of his childhood including afternoons when he cycled home from his father's herbal shop. Nwakaego would always call out to him from afar as he sped through the market.

"*Nwayo* Dalu.... what is chasing you boy?" asked an amused younger version of Nwakaego. At that time, she still had darker hair with just thin grey strands at the front as a promise of a soon greying hair in future

His twelve-year-old self would stop at her greeting; half panting. "I am late.... mama needs me to pound pepper for her, I do not want her to be angry." This was a routine they had formed with her always asking him even when she knew why he was in a hurry.

Coming towards him, she would pat his head while offering him a stuffed shopping bag. "Take some bread and a tuber of yam. Tell your mother that I send my greetings."

She had been his mother's only friend, and the only woman in the town besides his father that treated his mother like a human being. After the demise of his parents, she practically adopted him. Even though it lasted briefly, it would always be a beautiful period etched forever in his mind. To save her family's reputation he refused to hold on to her. It would have broken him if he had tainted her with the stigma that followed him all his life.

"It's been a while Dalu," offered Nwakaego when the silence stretched for too long. "I'm surprised that you even came here, seeing as you hate us all so much." There was no malice in her voice, she was just sad at how he turned out.

Instead of replying, Dalu patiently waited for her to attend to him so that he could be on his jolly way. He felt guilt wash over him when he noticed that her limping had worsened considerably since the last time that he saw her due to her arthritic knee. He was the one who usually gave her the herbs that provided temporal relief from the pain that it brought her.

Remembering that he brought a reliving medicine for her, he walked up to where she stood and set a wrapped parcel for her on the counter before looking up to see her waiting for him to speak.

"They will make you feel better. Sorry that I did not bring it sooner," he apologized and then straightened up. "Please, can you wrap up the usual stock I get? I did not bring a list, but my crops are yet to be harvested and I am... sorry that I just showed up, but it is urgent." He felt like a child all over again under her reprimanding gaze.

Nwakaego did not say anything but she offered him a seat which he took in the hopes that he would be hidden. He knew people waited outside refusing to enter because he was inside the shop; the marketers even went as far as refusing to sell to him except Nwakaego who had gone against them. If it had not been for her, he probably would have starved to death initially when the villagers had ostracized him.

He watched her as she threw out instructions to her sales attendant who hurriedly packed the bag of groceries for him. However, the bag was noticeably heftier than his usual order.

"Nwaka... I think that you over stocked for me... I said the usual."

Nwakaego turned to him and eyed him indifferently. "I'm aware of that. I heard the rumours Dalu, I am not prying but since you have an extra mouth to feed, I am making a concession."

He stared at her and scratched his beard indecisively. "It is not permanent, once she leaves... all this would be wasted." He had no intention of even asking her what the rumours were about because he knew what she was referring to.

"What makes you think that she would leave? Do you believe that everyone will leave you? Dalu, if you made it easier, I am sure they would stay." She stopped speaking only because her lips quivered, "you're not the boy I watched grow up... this person I am forced to see every time is nothing like my handsome put-together Dalu."

Her words and the tears gathering in her eyes only made his present state too obvious. He remained quiet, refusing to answer her. She turned away from him when she realised that he had no reply to her words choosing to busy herself once again by overseeing what was being added into his shopping bag.

A few moments later, she handed the bag over to him. "The second bag is free Dalu," she told him.

When he dared to argue with her, she almost used her walking stick on his head. Subdued, he grudgingly brought out the money as he eyed her imprudently.

He would have departed immediately, but she stopped him again. "You may have succeeded in erasing all your good memories, but I still remember them Dalu, you are one of my sons whether you acknowledge it or not. I just need you to be careful. Please forgive yourself for the past and move on. I am begging you." Having said her peace, she turned away from him not wanting to risk the chance of him rejecting her all over again.

"Not everyone is as brave as you *nne nwa,*" he replied surprising her. He left without a backward glance.

Nwakaego stood in that spot watching after his disappearing figure. Dalu even as an unkempt mess was still able to carry himself gracefully. Fate had played a cruel gamble with him and from the looks of things; won. He was now a shelled replica of the brave rebellious man she raised.

*

His words stung. He was just like every other person who saw her as a burden. She knew that she was wrong for baiting him last night when he had brought her food, but his words had gone straight to the core. Simdi was reminded once more, that no place was ever welcoming enough for her to settle. The minute she saw him walking out of this house, she took her small bag and ran. This was by far, the most foolish decision she had ever taken especially since her leg was not healed completely however, the sooner she left; the easier she would feel. She had survived this long without help, which was why she believed that she could endure this pain and dizziness. The dog barked loudly at her as she continued walking, but she ignored it. Her determination was fuelled by the assumption that she was saving Dalu. He was a good man, who should not be burdened by her. She was saving him; she was sure that after a while even he would see that she was nothing but trouble.

*

Dalu was greeted by silence and emptiness upon his return home; it was apparent that Simdi was gone. He scoffed bitterly calling himself a fool for expecting that she would stay back at the slightest opportunity to be free of him. He always knew that she would leave eventually. After all, she must have been going somewhere when he found her, but he did not expect that it would hurt him this much. The knowledge that she fled at the first chance stung, but after a moment of placating his barking dog he concluded in irritation that she was a foolish girl. If he were in her position, he would have waited until he was strong enough to embark on a journey before leaving. Instead, she had left in a weakened state from not eating and with an incapacitating wound. There was no way she would make it far without infecting her wound or worsening her physical state. She also had no sense of direction around the tricky terrains of Umi. Anything could happen to her; she could encounter bandits who would not hesitate to harm her or worse, spirits that would kill her and feast on her flesh. She was leading herself to death.

He sighed angrily as he sat on the wooden stool outside; his bag of foodstuffs forgotten in a corner. He was torn. "What should I do?" he demanded pulling his dreadlocks while his dog observed him helplessly. "I should just let her die," he declared angrily. Anyone who came across him at that very moment could easily conclude that he was truly a lunatic because no sane man talked to his dog.

The dog left his side as it sniffed the ground until it reached the gate before rushing back to Dalu. It pulled at his trouser hem as if it was beckoning Dalu to follow it. Dalu complied and stood concluding that he would not let any harm to come to her on his watch. If she still wanted to leave when he caught up with her, then he would lead her to the path that would keep her safe.

*

Her whole world was spinning in the darkness. She could hear every sound around her as fear and weakness overtook her senses. She experienced bouts of dizziness unlike anything she was accustomed to. Her legs throbbed so painfully that she had long since discarded being quiet in her movements. At some point nausea overtook her, and she slumped under the withering tree along the narrow path in an attempt to gather her bearings. She was beginning to realise that she may have acted too rashly in her moment of panic. She had left without food or water to at least sustain her. As she readjusted herself to a better sitting position, she sighed at her swollen leg.

Looking up to the sky she realised that she was alone out here in the dark night. The stars cast dim luminance over her, and she found herself idly counting them as a way of redirecting her mind away from what Dalu's reaction would be upon discovering that she had taken off. If it were her; she would be angry. She had acted like an ingrate but when she had made the decision, she was convinced that leaving Dalu was the wisest action to take. The man without saying too much had gone through pain; it was apparent by the way he chose to live. She was pain; the places she had been to and the people she had cared about could attest that they were eventually cursed with her pain. It did not matter that his intentions were good towards her, it would only be a matter of time before what had caused her to flee all those times would ultimately catch up to her.

She closed her eyes reminiscing on the first pain she had brought to a loved one. She was eleven at that time and her childhood friend *Ndubisi* had been twelve when they went for their normal swim inside the river of *ndi mmiri*. It was the last time she ever saw him because the next day he died, and she was the only one who knew why. On that fateful day, a beautiful woman appeared inside the river as they swam and had beckoned her to follow. She was caught in a trance and found herself swimming towards the vixen's outstretched hands. It was *Ndubisi* who saved her by holding onto her as though his very life depended on it. She remembered the woman's dark eyes as she cast it on poor Ndubisi; it was a look that promised vengeance. If she had listened and followed, there was a possibility that her friend would have still been alive. Even though no one blamed her for his death, the guilt of the whole incident still tormented her for all these years. Her reminiscing was halted by the presence of tired slumber.

At that moment with the silence of the night and the darkness that encompassed it, an ominous presence lay in wait watching her intently.

*

Not many things scared Dalu. He was occasionally scared of snakes because of their venom and most certainly, he was wary of time because he could not control it. His fear of life stemmed from how unpredictable it could be. This night proved that there was something else that could scare him, and it was the safety of Simdi. As he stood a distance away from the *tree of death* with his heartbeat increasing alarmingly, he knew that he was about to enter a sinister scene. As a child, he remembered the folklores told by his mother of the creature who was the embodiment of the tree. The tree was called that name for a reason because anyone who stepped a foot near it died; there were no two ways about it. Standing in shock, he stared at Simdi sleeping carefreely under it. He ignored the sense of foreboding within him as he slowly began advancing towards her. He rummaged through his memories of all the myths he had heard and how this knowledge could save them both. Before he could speak to Simdi or even yell at her to leave the place, he saw *the being*. She took the form of an old bent woman with scanty grey hair pulled back tightly behind her head. Her torso covered in nothing from head to waist, revealed her sagging breasts and age shrivelled dark skin. Unlike most old women he had encountered outside Umi who carried the presence of wisdom and comfort around them, this one was different. She reeked of evil, from her bloodshot hooded eyes to the slow ominous way she moved with intent. She was the main antagonist in almost all the stories of his childhood about the *onwu* tree that had haunted him in his dreams at night. It was told that for her to remain alive, she constantly fed on the life energy of unsuspecting victims that rested upon her tree. Her preferred victims were especially young girls.

The glaring glint of a knife tied in red cloth, brought Dalu out of his fear-induced stupor as he witnessed the woman attempt to stab Simdi who was still deep in her slumber. With intent, she aimed it directly for Simdi's heart however, his dog in its moment of bravery rushed towards the woman and viciously bit her on the leg which dislodged the attack. In spite of this, she managed to graze Simdi's shoulder which immediately woke her. Fortunately, by this time Dalu was already close enough to see her clearly. Gazing upon the woman for the first time, Dalu could not deny that she was in no simple words, ugly. She returned his open stare with a mouth twisted in a snarl. She said nothing and instead turned back to focus on Simdi who screamed in horror from the pain the woman had inflicted on her. The woman pounced on her again with a strength uncharacteristically surprising for someone her age.

Dalu at that moment spared no thoughts to consider his actions as he charged towards the woman driven by startling instincts to protect Simdi. He grabbed the woman and threw her off Simdi whose gown was already stained with her blood from her stab wound. Undeterred, the woman rushed back to them raising the knife again but this time aiming it for Dalu who quickly dodged and twisted it out of the shrieking woman's hand. He took the knife away from her, and in turn stabbed it into the tree. The woman groaned in pain as her eyes narrowed with malice. She pounced on him trying to remove the knife from the tree, but he stood his ground pushing her away with as much strength as he could muster.

"You will die... I promise you," she threatened digging her long sharp nails into his forearms.

He flinched but remained rooted at the spot where he plunged the knife deeper into the tree, while Simdi took refuge behind him in fear. As a child, he had heard that this tree was the source of her powers. The desperate look on the heaving woman's face confirmed that this particular myth was true. She watched the tree dejectedly, and on closer look, Dalu discovered that she was bleeding from the same middle spot where the tree oozed out thick red sap.

"Who are you?" she demanded angrily as she staggered back from him and fell to her knees.

He ignored her question knowing that his name was his greatest weapon. If he uttered a word of it to her, she would twist his mind to do her bidding.

Almost imploringly she spoke to him again as her eyes focused on Simdi, "it is this girl that I seek, I have no business with you... let me have her heart, and I will bless you with riches beyond your imagination."

Dalu snarled at her, his eyes narrowing at what she had just told him. She returned the gesture full on, and when she saw him pull out the knife, she charged at him again but was immediately rendered immobile when he dug the knife deeper into the tree making her stumble mid-step and fall on the ground.

"If you even attempt to look at her, I will stab you as much as I can, till you die. Do you hear me?" he commanded hoping that he could torture her enough to back down.

The woman writhed on the ground in pain, "you win, ...you win. I will do as you say," she groaned desperately. Simdi and the dog remained quiet although she was starting to feel dizzy again and this time, she was sure that it was because of her shoulder wound which continued to bleed.

"Make an oath!" He demanded, knowing that the witch's oath was the only guarantee they had that she would never search out Simdi after this night.

The woman used her sharp nails to draw blood from her wrist. "I *Onwu* swear this night that I will never set my eyes on her again till she dies," she swore frantically.

Dalu motioned for Simdi to leave, while the woman knelt there breathing tiredly. Her wicked eyes followed him angrily because he had foiled her evil intent, but the oath she had just taken prevented her from acting any further. When her eyes landed on his left wrist, a realization came to her at the sight of the white distinct coral beads wrapped around it.

"Ah, I see... it is you oh cursed child," mocked the witch triumphantly as her eyes landed on Simdi, she bared her blackened teeth before declaring. "You are of no use to me. Your blood would have tainted me because just by association with this cursed man you are cursed as well. You would have been better off as my meal than with him."

Her words were not alien to Dalu; he had heard them repeatedly from anyone who crossed his path. As they cautiously retreated from the tree refusing to turn their backs to her, he refused to acknowledge the heaviness in his chest at what her words implied.

*

The path back home was dark but Dalu knew the directions by memory. They were careful not to make too much noise because Umi was a land where spirits and creatures of the night roamed. They did not say a word until they were inside his compound. He held her hands carefully and led her quietly into the room she had run from. He left her only to return with a bowl of cold water, herbs, and a towel he would use to clean her wounds. He waited a while to gather his thoughts before he approached her; the truth was that he was waiting for her to run from him. If a witch could reject him, who could fault a normal girl for doing the same as well? He pulled the stool forward and sat down before reaching for her injured leg, which was covered in dirt and dried blood. Almost delicately, he raised the limb and kept it on his laps proceeding to wash off the dirt first. When he looked up at her, she sat staring at him as though she was seeing him for the first time. Initially, he thought that her silence meant that she was momentarily paralyzed from the shock of the events that had just taken place, but now as he looked into her eyes, he saw how her tear-filled hazel eyes seemed to stare into his very soul. He looked away as he applied the crushed antiseptic herbs into the wound. Luckily there was no infection and it would heal nicely if she did not aggravate it with her rash decisions.

"You need to take off the gown so that I can dress the wound on your shoulder," he informed her. He stood and left to bring another bowl of water. When he came back the dress was removed, and she was covering herself with a thin wrapper.

The temptation to say something snarky as he saw her flinch when he got closer was inching dangerously close to his lips, but he refrained from it because she was in a lot of pain. As he cleaned off the blood on the wound, he discovered that it was mostly superficial and would not require too much aftercare, so he just applied the herb into it and moved away from her. He fought against his treacherous mind from thinking of how soft her skin felt underneath his fingers.

"Were you afraid?" she asked him suddenly, and he stopped gathering what he came into the room with.

He looked at her indifferently and nodded, "I was more afraid for you then I was for myself, I am a man accustomed to the supernatural occurrences in Umi thanks to my late mother, but you Simdi have no idea what would have happened if I did not come. You would have died."

It might have been his words that broke her brave front but, before his very eyes she began to shed tears. It was not the loud sort of cry that anyone could hear; it was the type of private indulgence mastered by one who cried too often in silence. "I thought I was saving you... every time people get close to me, they suffer. I'm sorry that I acted so childish and I promise that if I decide to leave, I won't do it so ungratefully," she said holding herself from sobbing.

Dalu's hard look softened at her apology and he sighed defeatedly, "get some rest Simdi. When tomorrow comes, we can revisit this." With that, he nodded at her and left her to sleep. What could he say to her other than that? His home was not a prison, *she was free to come and go as she wished.*

4

Truce...

*L*ong lashes, furrowed brows, and the familiar *feeling of pain.* Simdi groaned opening her eyes hesitantly because of the unwelcome rays of sunlight evading her sleeping. She jolted awake at the remembrance of yesterday's events and grunted in pain as the wound reminded her of the role she played, in their unfortunate circumstances last night.

Gently she descended back into a lying position and briefly allowed herself to be distracted by the crocked line of ants climbing across the brown ceiling above her. Her shoulders which hurt badly was accompanied by stinging stiffness. Amidst all this, her stomach growled loudly as a reminder that she was famished. She knew without a doubt that she was now forever indebted to Dalu. As she watched him tend to her wounds yesterday without reprimanding her or getting angry, her heart had swelled in guilt for having put him through that ordeal because of her impulsiveness.

A shiver ran down her spine at the thought of the revolting old woman who had attempted to eat her heart yesterday. If Dalu had not decided to search for her, she would be dead. Death was not an option for her, she had to live in order to justify her mother's untimely passing.

Something else nagged at the back of her mind following what the old woman said to her. What did she mean by she was '*cursed* by association? Simdi did not have the right to point fingers at this man who constantly surprised her with his protection of her. He had fought to save her last night without caring that he was endangering his own life. She sighed tiredly deciding that the statement was null and void; Dalu was a compassionate man who she owed her life to. Instead of judging him, she would rather help him in any way she knew how before she left him.

When she watched him yesterday through the eyes of the moonlight, the tenderness with which he had handled her made her realise that he was wrongly misrepresented. Rather than the villain, Dalu was just a man in a lot of pain. It was in his brooding eyes and the carefulness that he used in making sure that he did not show her too much. He was unacknowledged and mistreated by others which in turn pushed him to live in seclusion. He was a man who had decided that he had no one to live for, and thus gave up on trying to do anything to fit in. She wondered what happened in his life to get him to this point where he currently was.

*

The movements in Simdi's room alerted Dalu that she was awake, but he remained in his workshop. After a few minutes, his compassionate side caved in and he decided to prepare a meal for her. It was almost two days since she last ate, and God forbid that she starved to death in his home. He was honestly annoyed with himself for being so considerate towards her, it was not like he forced her not to eat or run away. She made the decision herself, but he still felt compelled to ease her pain. It rattled his pride on how he broke his rules for her and had even felt sorry for her yesterday when she cried. She was the cause of the pain he felt in his arms from the scratches the witch inflicted on him, and she was also the cause of the break in his solitary life. It was because of her that he encountered a real-life witch yesterday for the first time. Ironically, none of the pain or confrontation with the witch mattered. All he had cared about in that moment was her safety.

He was surprised when he heard her coming towards the kitchen. He tried to look as indifferent as he could manage. There was no point hanging her stupidity and ungratefulness over her head.

"I went to your room and I didn't see you," she explained leaning on the wall as if her life depended on it.

She looked so frail and her lips were almost white from dehydration and hunger. He immediately offered her a cup of clean drinking water from the container beside him. She took it with shaky hands and drank it greedily indicating that she wanted more. He filled the cup again, and then set a stool for her to sit down outside the kitchen, away from the cooking smoke.

"Did you need anything?" he asked as she sat down after she had handed the empty cup back to him.

She looked down at her small slender fingers, wringing it nervously. "Dalu, I know I have said that I am sorry about last night, but I mean it even this morning. I really thought I was doing the right thing by leaving even though I was also annoyed. You surprised me by what you did last night, no one fights for me ever except my... my mother and I just want to tell you that I won't run again. You should never worry that if you leave, I won't be around when you return."

There was something in her voice; a vulnerability that Dalu had recognised the other day even when she fought so hard to hide. Today, it was presented to him without shame; he sighed offering her a plate of fried eggs and white bread. He sat on the steps and shrugged before replying.

"I never meant what I said to you that night...about regretting that I saved you. I was provoked and caught unawares by your attitude, so I acted on instincts. I do not regret that I brought you here. As you can see, there are things about me that normal people do not do, but it is who I am. I get angry and occasionally anxious, but I never regret a decision once I have made it. I admit that I was frustrated when you left yesterday without even taking your crutch to support your leg, but that was because I worried for you. You are free to leave at any time you deem fit to do so. In fact, when you feel that you can embark on your journey, I will personally lead you to where you will find safe passage. Do not act so unthinkingly from now on because it also affects me for the duration of time you are here."

When he was finished with what he wanted to say, silence settled back between them as Dalu watched her, surprised that he said all he did. This was the most he had spoken in years, but he did it to get his message across. Simdi swallowed, giving him an understanding nod, "thank you."

Nothing was said again as both of them ate their breakfast in silence. The dog sensing a truce had been reached, decided to make her appearance and Dalu fondly handed it a portion of breakfast smiling at it. It had been partly the dog's sense of smell that led him to Simdi. It was the first time he smiled in front of her, and almost self-consciously he wondered if his face looked right or disfigured because she stared at him unabashedly.

"It deserves thanks too," he said out loud looking at her with amusement in his eyes. Simdi immediately nodded smiling for the first time since she came out to the kitchen.

"Thank you, big guy" she whispered touching the brown and white head of the dog.

"Girl, she is a girl...not a guy," he corrected standing up and taking the plates inside.

When he turned, she was still sitting there watching him as he set the washed plates.

"If it's ok with you I can help you with your chores. I don't want to be a liability and also, I would feel better if I did so. I make a good meal once in a while... and I am very reliable with house chores...so..."

He considered her offer and tried to speak as thoughtfully as someone like him could manage. "It is not that I do not want you to help but... I mean look at you. You can barely stand Simdi. I will allow you to do so when you have healed. It will give me enough time to get accustomed to the change and..." He stopped talking conflicted with words on how best to say the next thing he wanted to voice out.

"Dalu... is there something I should not do when I start cleaning the house?" she asked watching him attentively. He nodded and started walking towards the house.

"Just one thing, do not change how things have been kept in the house. No matter how unsightly it looks, it is how I am. I do not like change." He left her there, without turning because he knew all he would be faced with were questioning eyes.

***

The River Temple

A long time ago, the servants of the river deity foretold the story of an ancient being that resided in the sacred springs in the village. These springs were protected by tall palm trees wrapped around the premises. It was told that only the worshippers and priests of the river could enter the sacred place; ordinary people who dared to venture there disappeared forever.

Today a middle-aged woman walked barefoot through the untrodden path holding an egg between her left thumb and middle finger. She was dressed in the official white silk kaftan and red turban tied on her head as a symbol of recognition for river priestesses in the village. The traditional *nzu* decorated her face in swirly symbols representing the motion of the river, while the black substance of *otangele* highlighted her dark eagle sharp brown eyes. Her skin which was a bronzed caramel revealed different beautification tattoos on her arms and back; they symbolized her strong affiliations to the river. She held a single palm frond in her painted black lips. As she approached, she chanted ancient songs taught to her by her predecessors and almost in timed accuracy flung the egg into the river. The egg was no ordinary egg as it was the white shelled egg of a python. Her followers who were already waiting on top of the smooth rocks scattered inside the river began shouting incantations as their white garments glistened in the water. Suddenly mist appeared around the foot of the spring, acting as a veil which prevented them from seeing what lay within the spring.

When the priestess called upon her spiritual eyes, she was faced with inhumane blue vertical pupiled eyes of the river goddess watching her with so much intensity that goose-bumps spread through her whole skin as she fearfully bowed her head. As a servant of the river, she had been taught not to show fear towards the creature she served, but no matter how many times she had performed this service; she never stopped cowering with apprehension. Only the gods knew what resided behind that veil; she had no intentions of finding out because no one who saw it lived to tell the story. From ancient myths and folktales, it was believed that the river goddess was a creature with the upper body which held beauty beyond any living creatures' imagination. It was so mesmerizing that it could not be merely spoken of. However, her beauty was juxtaposed by the lower body of a grey sea python which stood for her true nature.

Gathering every ounce of courage, the priestess offered her praise, "The great *Onwummiri,* your servants pay homage to your greatness." The rest of her followers who were already bowing their heads cried out in unified praises. Immediately a strong gusty wind pushed her face deeper into the water almost drowning her.

The goddess was not impressed. "Why have you come here?" she demanded in a thunderous voice.

"Forgive me oh great mother, command me so that I shall do as you wish," pleaded the priestess.

The goddess shrieked out again this time like a provoked animal. "Bring me my vessel and only then shall I bless your village. If she is not found, the days I protected the lives of your people will be over; I shall plague the river village and all its inhabitants." With that vow, the mist disappeared leaving no hint of the goddess.

As the servant of the river rose from her kneeling position, she trembled. The girl in question had evolved into an intelligent prey since she escaped captivity. The female teacher had foolishly sacrificed her life for the girl to escape and ever since then, the girl had disappeared whenever they were close to locating her. She had also avoided rivers which made it harder to locate her essence. The priestess sighed;

the sooner she was found, the faster disaster would be averted. She had never heard the goddess so angry.

*

Dalu's life depended on routines and one was starting to form between him and Simdi. With Simdi regaining her health, she became a useful addition to his home. In the morning before he woke up, his whole compound would be swept; the dusty surfaces in his house wiped off, and the cobwebs around the corners carefully swept away. The second routine was that she stayed out of his personal space making sure that she was done with her chores before he even woke up. He always heard when she was cleaning his compound but as he stirred, or about to wake up she would return to her room, only coming out when he had gone to sculpt his wood. The third routine was the fact that she took care of the cooking. He was no longer the one who fed her, instead, she made it her personal conviction to nourish him. She had lied about her experience in cooking. It was not good, it was fantastic. The taste of her food was so overwhelming to him that the first time he tasted it, he almost disgraced himself by licking the plate clean just to make sure that no leftover remained. He refrained from doing so, but who would blame him? Having been accustomed to the taste of his own food for the past six years, the difference in the taste of another person's varied method of cooking caught him unawares. It was the first time that he had no intention of sharing the food with the eager dog that devoured the leftovers greedily. If this was the sort of results that would be yielded by letting her take over, then, by all means, he would not stop her.

*

It had been two weeks since Simdi had come to Dalu's home. While things were no longer awkward between them, there was still emptiness in their interactions. She was upholding her promise of not bothering him. However, today as she brought out her small laundry, she decided to help him out as well. The thing about Dalu was that while he seemed unperturbed by his unkempt and unhygienic appearance, he maintained a certain level of orderliness in his home. In addition to that, these days he was considerate towards her because he no longer wore those dirty torn shirts and trousers; he made conscious efforts to clean his face, brush his teeth, and bound his dirty dreadlocks. It did not solve the problem entirely, but she appreciated his effort. As part of her goodwill, she decided to also wash his clothes for him. The minute she saw him leaving the gate, she immediately rushed to his room and carried all the piled-up clothes to the back of the house. This was not breaking that one rule he had asked her; she was doing it for his own good.

*

Dalu halted from raising the curtain to his room. It was odd that it was illuminated because he had been away all afternoon. Squinting curiously, he could make out the silhouette of Simdi. He was not sure how to react to the fact that she was inside his room this late into the night. He was tired from his business journey to sell his art which had taken longer than expected. All he wanted to do was to collapse on his bed and enjoy his well-deserved rest. The minute he stepped into his room; he knew that something had changed. His dirty clothes were no longer in the pile where he left them. Instead, they were all folded into a basket close to his bathroom door. Even the smell in his room had changed into a lemon type of fragrance that he could not pinpoint where it was emitting from.

"What have you done?" he demanded, making no effort to hide the displeasure in his voice.

Simdi jumped up, startled by his presence. "Oh... I um ... well, I was doing my laundry and yours were just lying there, so I thought I would just do all of them since you've been busy with your sculptures. You don't need to worry, I made sure that I got most of the stains out and even used lemongrass to add fragrance to it," she explained sounding very pleased with herself.

Dalu's head began spinning as anxiety rapidly washed over him. "You thought? I asked you for one thing...did I tell you that I needed your help... you do not know what you have done. You have doomed me," he shouted pulling his hair in a frenzied manner as he began pacing in circles. *She had doomed him!*

For six years Fate had left him alone because he had not changed from the gutter rat it wanted him to be. His obedience to the will of Fate had saved him from further misery. Fate had left him because he had become something that could never attract its jealousy. Simdi changing his dirty clothes into clean fresh smelling clothes was an invitation of Fate's contempt.

"Why... why... why...," he kept repeating as he crumbled unto the ground breathing too fast for him to handle. He was suffocating in his fear and anxiety. Who would Fate take from him as punishment this time, Nwakaego? His Dog? Or was it Simdi? What could he give this time to save them? He had nothing else to give...Nothing.

"Dalu... please tell me what is wrong...you are scaring me please." He could hear Simdi's concerned voice accompanied by loud ringing sounds in his ears. He clutched his chest in pain trying to breathe, but he was suffocating. Everything went dark.

*

Simdi had never seen a panic attack first-hand, but she had heard about of it from a classmate who experienced it. Due to its rarity in her small village; everyone likened it to being possessed. However, after she confirmed that he was still breathing, she immediately ran into his bathroom and brought a damp towel which she assumed was his and cleaned the sheen of sweat on his forehead. She was perplexed at what she must have done that could incite such a reaction from him.

"Dalu...please just breath," she begged in a shaky voice while she watched him taking laboured breathes. It had not been her intention to cause him this much panic. She had done what she did because she wanted to help him. "Please just breathe" she repeated and bravely held his hand. She was surprised when he tightened his hold enough for her to see that he was struggling in his unconsciousness. She kept repeating that he breathed and somehow, he heard her. Eventually, his breathing evened out and he fell asleep holding on to her.

*

They were running in a maize field. A couple who dressed in simple white cotton fabrics and held three adorable young children; two boys and a beautiful girl. The tall dark well-built man had long shoulder length dreadlocks which was styled neatly in a ponytail, a groomed beard, and laughter- filled eyes. His wife was a beautiful woman with an oval face, kind eyes, dimpled cheeks, and a curvy figure accentuated in the white dress she wore. They wore no shoes, but they did not care.

"Dalu... do you think that we will touch the sun?" she asked him her eyes gleaming with love for him.

Dalu smiled as he held up her hands and kissed it tenderly, "if that is your wish, then I promise we will touch it." He could not bear to tell her that their love was too ambitious; anyone who got too close to the sun; burned.

***

Dalu was pulled out of his unconsciousness by the sound of his dog's lazy barking outside. Looking around he saw Simdi sitting beside him as she watched the moon from the opened window. When he looked down, he saw that their hands were intertwined. He released it immediately as though such a touch burned him. She turned to him and watched him wearily.

"What happened to you...I have heard of it before; it is called a panic attack. It is what happens when fear possesses the mind and overwhelms it with lies," she told him boldly.

"I do not wish to speak about it. I also need you to leave my room," he told her coldly leaning on the nearest wall tiredly. She had no idea of what she was talking about, he was within his rights to be afraid. Who was she to put a name to his reaction as though it was an ailment?

To his surprise, she stood and walked up to him where he leaned on the wall with his eyes closed. She touched his forehead first and then her fingers moved downwards to firmly hold his jaw, forcing him to look into her mesmerizing eyes. He remained motionless in shock of her proximity as he registered the spicy flowery scent that surrounded her.

"You are Dalu, a man who took a stranger on the night it rained so heavily, you are also the man who battled a witch and won... you will not succumb to fear. It will not rule you," she declared and released him. She left his room without as much as a backward glance.

Dalu remained in that spot mouth hanging open at how assertive she had been with him. It reminded him of bull tamers in Umi, who rode bulls to submission. She had that same look in her eyes; no vulnerability, no fear, no malice. It was a confident look that spoke words she believed in. Dalu remained seated in that position all night as he replayed what had happened. By the time morning began to break, a tiny portion of his mind that was not overridden with the fear of Fate had awoken from Simdi's words. *Fear would not rule him.*

5

Sounds....

*T*hump, thump, thump... the sounds of the heavy axe chopping wood deep inside the forest reverberated.

Dalu stilled and wiped his sweat-sheened face with his forearms. His whole arms were sore, but he was determined to chop the required amount for his next work. Judging by the darkening sky, he knew that it was already getting late and he needed to return home in time to eat Nwakaego's delicious dinner. He heard dry grasses and twigs behind him crunching from hesitant footsteps that drew close to him. He continued his task ignoring it but at the same time, he prepared his stance in case it was a surprise attack from some of the malicious boys his age that placed bets on who would finally win him in a fight. He knew what he represented in Umi; a forbidden fruit that tempted people who despised him. He was a handsome young agile man who effortlessly captivated the hearts of young girls and women that dared to desire him in the village. His tall height and well-defined physique complemented his smooth ebony skin. In addition to that, his mysterious and rebellious nature only added to the allure surrounding him; it made him a subject of interest.

The footsteps stopped, and he held his breath waiting for a possible confrontation. None came and instead he heard a soft uncertain feminine voice from behind him.

"Why do you always cut wood?"

Letting out the breath of relief he held, he turned and saw *Kaima*. He knew her; she had been the only one who visited him when his parents died, even when the villagers refused to show him any sympathy. She was a beautiful young woman with a fairer brown complexion than he had ever seen in the village; it looked like soft warm honey. She was not slender but instead had curvy hips, a tiny waist, and ample breasts. This close to her, he could see the attractiveness that prompted many young men of his peerage to preposition her for courtship and marriage. On top of that, she was the first daughter of the richest man in the village aside from the king. Someone like her did not have any business meeting him in a place like this, it would taint her image.

"I use them for my sculptures," he answered dismissively turning back to his task. The whole place suddenly felt too compact and Dalu grew self-conscious especially because he could feel her eyes steadily observing him. He suddenly felt an impulse to gather his dreadlocks that fell on his face, it was curled and tangled to the point that he forewent taming it with a comb. Usually, he would have put more effort into grooming it by cutting it short as his father did, but the thought of his late father only brought back bad memories of his past. Ignoring it ensured that those memories remained buried in unconscious oblivion.

He heard her sigh loudly before speaking, "I like how quiet it is inside here, it's so serene. It could be a great spot for meditation... do you meditate?" she asked almost timidly attempting again to start a conversation with him. Her purpose for doing that was still unknown to him, but he did not react to her question.

After a noticeable attempt at ignoring her, he stopped chopping again and turned to observe her contemplatively recalling her insightful words. Most girls in Umi did not know what meditation was. The most they cared about was settling down with a man who would pump them with his offspring. Kaima on the other hand, spoke poetically exuding clearly her passion for nature. It was in that moment that his opinion of her changed, she was no longer the rich man's daughter... he now saw the '*who*' rather than the '*what*' in her person.

"Tell me Kaima, how is it that a girl like you knows what meditation means? This is no insult; to be frank I have not heard anyone ask me that question," he explained ceasing his activities altogether. She now had his full attention which rarely happened. Dalu was not a person who took notice of people, but this girl was someone he wanted to hear about.

She offered him a smile so sad that he almost retracted the question. "When I was a child, my mother was a spiritualist. She understood and was immersed in nature. She taught me how to relax my mind until all I felt was a keen awareness of my core being. I only started coming here in recent years."

Dalu nodded at her, visibly impressed again and he did not attempt to hide it this time. "Yes, I meditate also but I do not come here always, because of the night creatures and wild animals. Why do you risk so much by coming here?" He had only asked it out of concern for her safety. It did not occur to him that the question would open up old wounds.

She briefly closed her eyes, as if she was picking out the right words to best convey her answer and when she opened her eyes a sad expression flickered momentarily on her pretty face, "there is no peace in my life outside this forest. My ... stepmother prefers me away from her presence and my father... he does not protest for me."

As he studied her, Dalu was reminded of a candle almost burning out. It all made sense now how he knew her even before she had offered her condolences. A memory of a younger version of Kaima flashed in his mind as she knelt next to a mango tree not too far from his family home. He had been a twelve-year-old boy unable to ignore a crying child deeply affected by raw anguish from the loss of her mother who had died in childbirth. He was returning from the herb fields with his father when they saw her. His father had comforted her and convinced her to return to her home. It was a shame he did not remember her after that day until now, maybe he would have been nicer to her. Everyone in Umi knew of her unfair maltreatment in the hands of her favoured stepmother and her father's blatant disinterest towards her.

"You have suddenly gone quiet; did I reveal too much to make you uninterested after all?" she asked him wearily.

Dalu remained quiet suddenly overcome with shame and reproach at how he treated her on the day when she had offered her condolences to him following the death of his parents. She had bravely ignored the commands to isolate him and had visited him. Dalu who was wallowing in anger and grief at that time was horrible to her.

"I am here for you because I understand," she had said to him in an attempt to console him, but all he heard that evening was the pity in her voice despite her good intentions. Those words for a few minutes had even given him brief comfort, but then his vulnerability allowed him to doubt her. He believed that a girl like Kaima was giving him false hope; how could a blueblood understand an outcast like him?

"You are wicked as they are," he accused her laughing dryly. "Even in my grief you mockingly offer me false hope. At least others do not hide behind kindness. You would prefer that I believe you before you ruined me," he spat out angrily and the shock on her face only incited him further. "Get out! Get out with your lies and cruel words. Leave me to my grief... leave me!" he shouted dragging her out and shutting the door on her face.

Brought out of his remembrance, Dalu shook his head in a guilt-stricken stupor. "Kaima... I ..." What could he possibly say to mend the ungratefulness he displayed that day?

She cleared her throat and allowed him to see the tears filling her eyes, "I did not know what I had done that day... I...tried after then to ask what I said or did wrong and why you hated me so much, but I was too afraid of how you would react."

Dalu walked under a tree and sat down beckoning her to follow him. It was getting late and the evening had grown cold. When she took a seat as far from him as possible, he sighed dejectedly; she was truly afraid of him now. "I...was grieving and my mind told me that you gave me false hope. You are the daughter of *Akajiego*, why would you possibly want to comfort me if not to mock me?"

She looked hurt that he would assume that, "false hope? I would never do it. I have tasted abandonment Dalu, I would never abandon you like my father and everyone else have abandoned me. When I told you I understood, I really meant it. That pain, anger, and grief are emotions that no one is more attuned to than I who is forced to relive it every day that I exist as *Akajiego's* daughter."

Even now as he heard all she said, his mind was still plagued with mistrust and uncertainty. It did not make sense that Kaima wanted anything to do with him. Nonetheless at the same time, he sympathized with her and all that she had passed through in the hands of her family.

"Kaima, I am truly sorry that you are suffering but... I have nothing to offer you. I am an orphan who would have starved to death had it not been for my mother's best friend who took me in. Anyone who gets entangled with me will always be blackened...why do you insist even now to... to be associated with me?" She did not reply immediately but pointed to the sky. The moon hung above them, and one star shone brightly beside it, "Dalu, does that star cease to twinkle simply because the moon is also in the sky?" He shook his head reluctantly not understanding what she wanted to say.

"To me, watching you prove them wrong by surviving their hate every day is inspiring. You ...are the star that will never stop twinkling. The appearance of the moon does not eclipse how stunning your perseverance is.

What I am trying to say is that... I need you in my life...as my friend, as my confidant, as anything you can offer me... but I do not want to stay far away observing your light. I want ... to partake of it."

Dalu knew instantly that he did not stand a chance with Kaima. Even without trying, she had wrapped herself firmly by his side and in his heart. What could he possibly say that would be worthy of the praise she just showered him? What had he done to deserve it? It was at that moment, with only the moon and the stars as witnesses that he did what he believed was the only sane thing to do. He shyly moved towards her and placed his larger palm on her smaller one. She was waiting for an answer as tears rolled down her smooth cheeks. With his thumb, he caught it smiling encouragingly at her.

"Kaima," he whispered tenderly, "will you be my friend?"

She entwined their fingers together and smiled in relief, "yes and...more one day."

Dalu smiled too, feeling light-headed but he was not scared. Her confidence was endearing, and he vowed that he would treat her better than everyone who disappointed her in the past. He would treat her like the best gift in the world. On that significant night, their destined union came to be.

*

Dalu opened his eyes from the position that he sat inside his workshop. Looking around his workshop scattered in wood shavings, he wondered why he was remembering precious memories of Kaima. When she died, he had wanted to join her. It felt like it was his fault, he blamed himself and no one else. Why had he not been taken instead of her? Death had taken her without even a consideration to what she was leaving behind. Even though it hurt, he would never regret beginning that friendship with her. It had led to one of the best times in his youthful years.

His attention shifted from nostalgic thoughts to sweeping sounds outside, which immediately reminded him of the other person living in his home. Today made it the fifth day since he fainted in front of Simdi. They were yet to speak to each other, and she stopped sharing her meals with him. He expected himself to feel grateful for the silence, but it felt too empty in his home. It was almost a month since she lived with him, but this was the most interesting he had lived in the last six years. Now that companionship and care had re-entered into his life, he craved it selfishly even when he did not have the right to it.

Factors such as his unwavering distrust to change and her misguided belief in him continued to create this distance between them. Why did she believe that he was a strong man when he could not even save his family? He had given her every reason to confirm his madness. He was weak too; how else could he explain his extreme reaction to her consideration to wash his dirty clothes? Change only brought him problems and if he did not change; he would have peace. Why was this belief suddenly sounding implausible to him?

Dropping his chisel and mallet, Dalu decided to call it a day. As he approached the living room area, he realised that Simdi was no longer sweeping. Instead, she was busy in the kitchen; he did not approach her. That would come at another time. He went back into his room and picked up one of the shirts she washed for him. It looked out of place beside him and he dropped it on the bed deciding that he could at least clean himself just a bit today. It would not do him any good if he tried apologizing looking like he crawled out of garbage. Was it wrong to admit that he felt miserable since they stopped talking?

*

The delicious aromatic scent of Simdi's food floated into Dalu's room and he did not hesitate to leave his room. He wanted to catch her before she disappeared again, but to his greatest surprise, she was casually setting the plates on the small wooden dining table. He stopped in front of her and she looked up at him before focusing on her task.

"Are one of these plates mine? I want to eat with you," he announced awkwardly, and she nodded "Yes, I was going to call you when I was done."

Without waiting, he pulled out the chair at the head of the table and sat down eagerly watching her as though the process of setting a table was the most interesting thing in the world. Where was his pride? He was acting like a doting puppy; even his dog was not this eager to see him.

She eventually sat down and helped him dish out the quantity of the *jollof* rice that he could finish. He watched her as if he was seeing her for the first time. She looked better than he had ever seen her appear; having gained back the reasonable amount of fat for her to radiate health. Also, her face had filled out to reveal soft features, high cheekbones, and full pink lips.

As he continued observing her discreetly, he wondered why in the world had he concluded earlier that she was not beautiful? Simdi was one of the most beautiful women he had ever seen in a long time. Tonight, she looked extra nice in her yellow flower dress and hairpin placed on her short hair, which was starting to grow into a small afro. He could not stop sneaking looks at her even as he ate quietly. He felt uneasy at how silent everywhere was and he wanted to change it. It was not as if they always conversed, but a week ago they had formed a routine that reflected the level in which they progressed in terms of being accustomed to each other.

"You know that I appreciate what you do in this house. You do not have to, but you still do," he said in a bid to strike a conversation with her.

Simdi looked at him and nodded, but she remained quiet. He took that as a sign that she did not want to talk to him. Why then did she set the table to eat together? If she did not want him, she should have continued ignoring him. He was suddenly annoyed at how hurt he felt that she was sitting beside him but was still detached from him.

"Today you look better Dalu; less unkempt, oddly well put together in your own way." He did not reply her because he felt disheartened at her cool 'matter of fact' statement. It had taken a lot of mental assurance for him to towel his body, brush his teeth, gather his hair and change his cloth to get to the point he was. He was gradually changing but it seemed as if she was disappointed that he did not in one day magically become a charming man; it was not fair.

"If you have a problem with how I look then that is your problem... you have your own flaws, but I do not hold them against you." He made sure that she knew he was offended.

Simdi looked at him this time and said in a calm voice, "I don't hold them against you either. I never have, Dalu you know this. My silence isn't anger. It is respect for your personal space. I forgot my place for a second when I acted the way that I did. I forgot that I had no right to touch your things, nor did I have the right to ask you to suddenly overcome your deepest fears for me."

Dalu sighed but he was at a loss for words. He was about to talk when she stood up. "I made something for us," she explained with a bright smile on her face. Everything about her attitude this evening did not make sense, one minute she was treating him sternly, then soothingly, and now she was suddenly happy; he could not pinpoint exactly what the problem was. A few seconds later she came in holding a small pan of cake. Kaima had baked for the children and himself during their birthdays. It was six years since he ate cake; the scene was like déjà vu and he fought with himself not to remember all the times they celebrated precious moments in the privacy of this little paradise made specifically for only them.

Simdi sat back down and stuck a lighted candle into the middle of the round plain cake. With unfocused eyes, as though she was in another place altogether, she said, "today is my birthday...I turned ... 23." She kept quiet for a while, her eyes watering. "I've been running for a year now, I should call this my anniversary too, you know?" One dry laugh later she continued, "I really believed that as I left my mother behind, I would come back almost immediately with answers to our misfortune, but it's been one hurdle after the other. How unfortunate am I that my mother died on this same day? It's like no matter how much I fight to forget; this day serves as a reminder to me."

Dalu fought the urge to hold her even as she fought against herself not to spill her tears. Losing her mother on her birthday was indeed a terrible thing. He had no idea how to ease this pain away. "Simdi, tell me how I can help... I do not know what to do," he pleaded, involuntarily extending his hands to touch her, and then retracting it. He was in no position to hold her or touch her, but what then could he do. This young woman was hurting so much in her quiet mourning and he was helpless.

She shook her head, blowing out the candle before standing up slowly. "You know, I make the same wish every year." When she looked back at him, she allowed him to behold the sadness within her hazel depths. "Is it such a bad thing that I always wish that I had never been born?" Her question was left unanswered. "Goodnight Dalu," she said softly before retreating into her room.

He remained seated alone in the darkening dining table faced with an uncut cake. She was so young with all her life in front of her. She could be whatever she wanted and from what he had seen from his encounters with her; all she wanted was to be happy. However, the person who had just left was drowning in the sorrow that she bore alone. He cleared the plates and blew out the candles. He reached her room and stood outside waiting for signs of her crying; it never came. Simdi was too skilled in silent tears to give off the fact that she was grieving. Within him, he knew it was not right.

After his parents death, he had wept for days, and following the untimely demise of his wife and sons, he had sat down on the muddy ground and shed tears. It was not healthy to hold so much inside without release. Tonight, he knew what he would do for her; he would give her the gift of tears. No one understood the art of grieving as much as he did and the detrimental effects of holding in so much; just look at what he turned into. Simdi needed a final release of the grief she had kept locked deep within her and today he would help her find it. Tentatively, he raised the curtain and entered the room to see her huddled tightly inside the worn blanket. Cautiously, he went to the window and sat down on the stool as he glanced at the moon surrounded by twinkling stars.

"When I was twenty-three, I was already a father. I married when I was twenty; I had no clue what I was even doing. How was I going to feed my wife or the infant we had welcomed into the world? My parents died when I was sixteen. My father did not leave anything behind except for a useless field of herbs because he foresaw a long life with my mother, so there were no prior preparations for me to properly learn the profession of a healer. Simdi, I struggled in that first year after the marriage. My sculptures were not as good as they look now, no one would buy it and I was afraid that my wife Kaima would starve to death. My greatest fear was that I had failed her especially since she had already given up being the daughter of the richest man in Umi to marry me. She never complained but I knew she suffered. I held it all in my heart and did all the odd jobs I could find. It did not matter how degrading it was, as long as it paid, I did it. One day it was too much, we had an infant son who was sick. I had no money to take him to a health centre, but we were lucky that my adoptive mother *Nne nwa* stepped in to help us. She took one look at me barely hanging on and she pulled me into her arms. I broke down then, in front of everyone who could see. I wept so much that my head was spinning but when I stopped, I felt anew."

When he looked back at her, she was attentively watching him with tear-filled eyes from a sitting position. "Do you know why I told you this?" he asked, and she shook her head. Just as she had done to him not too long ago; he lifted her wobbling chin with his long fingers and looked deeply into her hazel eyes. "I want you to cry," he commanded. "I want you to shed the tears you have silently held in your heart all this time. I am speaking of that particular tears you held back when your mother died; I think it is time you let it out. It is only then that you can be able to cry about other things like tears of joy, tears of falling in love, tears of passion, and tears of comfort... so cry Simdi." He was shocked at how deeply he felt at his own words because they were true. He was not a hypocrite, so he did not tell her that things would get better but the words he just spoke now, he had cried for all those reasons.

He let her go and she closed her eyes breathing heavily as those silent sobs slowly became loud anguished cries. The only thing he could do was to remain by her side, which he did by sitting quietly beside her while he waited for her to free her burden. He wanted to hold her in his arms and hug her as tenderly as he knew he could, but he held back. He had no right to do it, but there was no harm done in offering her a presence that would not judge her or her vulnerability. A few seconds passed and then slowly she placed her head on his shoulder, staining the lemon fragranced shirt with long overdue tears. He patted her head soothingly. She was a mess of emotions; it did not mean that he thought less of her. Simdi trusted him with her tears; tears that she had not shed since her mother's death. She deserved to let it all out. They remained like this for minutes and then gradually the crying stopped.

Simdi sighed and spoke, "I saw the flour inside the cupboard... I doubt the cake will taste good; the flour could be stale. I wonder how it tastes." She looked up at him with red puffy eyes and tear stained face. Anyone would have immediately looked pitiful after crying so much but not Simdi; at this moment when she looked expectantly at him, all he thought was that she looked unrealistically appealing. Without saying anything, he held her hands and led her back to the table where the cake sat.

"Sit," he commanded softly and then brought a knife which he handed over to her before taking a seat opposite her. "You can judge for yourself," he whispered afraid to break the delicate moment he was witnessing.

She obeyed him and cut the cake, before tasting a small portion and making a face, "it's too flaky, did I forget to add something?" she asked rhetorically but continued eating. He joined her smiling secretly; it was the worst cake he had ever tasted, but he would never mind eating it if she offered it.

"Happy birthday," he told her leaning forward with his chin resting in his palm; to his surprise, she grinned slowly mirroring his position. "I've always wondered how old you were?" she admitted curiously.

Dalu raised one full brow and smirked, "Is that so? I must be interesting for a strong headed tyrant like you to be wondering about me," he replied jokingly. To his satisfaction, she chucked. When she stopped, he moved back slightly to put distance between them before revealing. "Thirty-two."

Simdi burst out laughing, "Are you sure? I mean even though there is a whopping nine-year age gap between us... I always pegged you for a man in his late forties."

He almost fell off his chair at her assumption; he did not look that old. She was lying, "take it back you malicious wretch," he said in mock offence.

Simdi waved him off, pleased that she got under his skin. "Ah, so you are vain...don't act so shocked old man, it's your fault for not taking good care of yourself."

They argued afterwards; mostly him accusing Simdi of her deteriorating eyesight, and how every human was vain but Dalu noticed the return of their comfortable companionship. Simdi was going to be fine. Her grief would heal, and one day if she was still around, she would witness the process of his change that was already in motion.

6

*P*hoebe appreciated living; she revelled in waking up every morning to the sunlight on her fair skin. She particularly loved the smell of pine trees outside her window, the taste of tea after she brushed her teeth, and the gowns she made for herself during weekends spent relaxing. Outside her home, she loved her job as a teacher and never regretted coming back to her hometown to impact on the lives of the younger generations. Giving everyone happiness and earning the respect of the villagers gave her a reason to live. These people had been there for her and her older brother when her parents had perished in a ghastly car accident; she had been a little girl when it happened. To top it all up, she was blessed with a wonderful fiancé who she was going to marry at the end of the month. She could not wait to be a wife; she would be an amazing mother whom loved her husband and children.

As she trekked down to the path that led to her small teacher's cottage, she saw a scooter parked in front of the compound. A man of average height sat outside her home waiting for her. He had a darker skin tone than hers, with a square face marred by a thin scar running from his left cheek down to his jaw. With familiar brown eyes, her brother offered her a welcoming smile. He was bulky just like their father while she resembled their mother who had been a petite woman and he was seven years her senior, but they were very close. This man had singlehandedly raised her and given her an education; she owed him everything. He rarely visited unannounced but all the same, she was happy to see him.

"Big brother, good evening. What brings you here?" she asked hugging him fondly when she reached him as he stood to receive her. There was something odd about his expression, he looked weary, but he continued to smile at her kindly.

He bent and offered her a bag filled with crops from his farm, which she accepted gratefully unlocking her door. "Harvest was great this month, so I decided to bring you a share... and also there is something that must be discussed urgently."

She went into the kitchen leaving him in her living room. She came out with a bottle of beer and a glass cup, which she set on the stool in front of him. While he poured the beer into the cup, she sat waiting and passed time by smoothening the wrinkles on her dress.

"Phoebe... I don't know how to say this," he said hesitantly looking remorseful.

She frowned confusedly, "are you well? How's your wife and my nieces? You are scaring me."

Her brother raised his hands and shook his head, "We are fine. In fact, it concerns you and the women in our lineage actually." He stopped and sighed, "When I was younger, mum left me with a task to relay this message to you...our women are guardians to the vessels of the river goddess."

Phoebe tried but failed to make sense of what her brother said, "river goddess? Come on *Okorie* that was an old wives' tale that mothers spun for entertainment in the moonlight. We are believers, we do not conform to things like that. You are not making sense." She was adamant that he would even say such an archaic thing. She always considered the idol worship in the village appalling, but she never voiced it out.

"Phoebe, this was left at my doorstep," he said dropping three palm frond leaves tied around the red fabric on the table. "It's my fault I agree, I should have told you about your heritage and the task ahead. I just wanted you to have the life I could not. I sacrificed everything I had so that you could pursue your dreams and I am so proud of you. However, Phoebe if you do not heed the summons of the river, we will all die. Our parents ignored it and perished. To save our lives I... I made a pact with the goddess that when the time was right, I would bring you for her to groom her vessel. It was the only way that we would have remained alive."

Phoebe stood angrily her heart beating in apprehension, "A pact? You made a pact with the devil... and you expect me to be complacent with it. I have my own life! My life as a married woman is starting by the end of this month. What do you want me to do?" She never raised her voice on her brother in her life, they never fought but she was very close to ushering him out of her home.

"You will live normally. You just have to nurture the vessel until she comes of age to assume her life as the goddess. Nothing will change Phoebe, but if you ignore this summon, we won't have much of a life. It is not superstition; I know what has happened to all who disobeyed. Those stories we listened to as children were all true. I beg you, Phoebe, to save our lives."

Her brother dropped on his knees pleadingly and Phoebe immediately went to him, "can I at least discuss it with *Obinna*?"

Her brother sighed and sat back. "The longer we hold off, the more pressing it becomes. Bear that in mind," he told her ominously as he stood up. "I will extend your greetings to my family. Come to the shop when a decision is reached." He left her after that.

Phoebe sat back closing her eyes. Had it been too early to conclude that her life was perfect?

*

Obinna was the love of Phoebe's life. She met him at the university, and they dated for seven years, although he wanted to marry her after one week of dating. His handsomeness was not what drew her to him. He could easily smile even when he was in so much pain. He was compassionate towards others and did not have one malicious bone in his body. He was tall, slender, and possessed the type of manly face that caused other women to turn when they were walking down the campus. Even after school ended, and he remained in town as an engineer; he never failed on his weekend visits to her. He supported her love for teaching and did his best to assure her whenever she met a dead end in her career goals. They were a team, a functional unit that she had grown to depend on.

It was a Friday and he was scheduled to walk into her door at any moment. She replayed how she would break the news to him. She stayed awake all night after her brother left and had thought of this all week. She would not let anything interfere with her life; she would look at it as a task. It would be like the times she marked the tests she gave her students; she would treat it like the scores she methodologically filled into blank sheets. All she needed was for Obinna to see it like that too; she was saving her family by accepting the role. However, if he protested even once she would fight with all she had to reject it. There were definitely other solutions, there had to be.

The minute her fiancé entered her home, all worrying thoughts were postponed. She ran up to him offering loving kisses. Many people frowned upon displays of affection between unmarried couples in this village, but she was a modern woman who did not abide by those rules; Obinna was worth it.

"I should stay away longer if you will welcome me like this," her fiancé joked lifting her up easily while she wrapped her shapely legs around his slender waist, and they kissed passionately. All the explanations she prepared disappeared when she looked into his eyes. The way he looked at her sometimes made her feel like she was the best thing that ever existed in his world. She wanted to be everything to him, his happiness, his inspiration, and his source of comfort, just as he was hers.

"I want every single part of you, *Obi m*," she whispered bringing their foreheads together. She could hear the beating of his loving heart.

"You have it," he replied huskily, and they resumed kissing. The kiss gradually changed from the soft gentle press of lips to a deeper hungry exploration which moved them almost desperately into her bedroom. They made passionate love and Phoebe wished things would stay this way forever. She knew they could still have their perfect life together.

*

The aftermath of their lovemaking was tranquil bliss as Obinna continued to shower her with peppered kisses. She smiled dreamily even though she had not slept a wink.

"Let's get married tomorrow Obi m?" she asked suggestively not sure she could wait for three weeks; she was so scared that he would not want her after she told him of her latest discovery. The kisses stopped, and she opened her eyes to see him watching her carefully. "What is it?" she asked him when he continued staring.

"I know you, Phoebe, something has you so worried. Even our lovemaking was different tonight. You were too intense...I could not help but feel that this was more significant than other times. I need to know what it is?" Her heart felt like it would burst for this man who loved her this much.

"Okorie visited me at the beginning of the week. He came on behalf of the river temple. They ... said that the women in our family are guardians to vessels of the river goddess. I will reject it, I told him I would, but he said with certainty that if I did, then all of us will perish. This is against all that I believe in you know this, but if there is a chance that it is true then it would explain the circumstances behind the death of my parents." When she did not hear a word from him, she desperately continued. "He promised that it would not interfere with my life. I just have to guide the vessel, but nothing will change with us... Please say something, my love," she begged already dreading the words that he would speak.

He stood instead, ignoring her attempt to keep him in the bed. When he turned to her, it was with extended hands reaching for her. "If this will save your life, then let's get married." She did not expect this reaction, but this was what mattered the most.

That night, a few miles outside the village amidst the disapproval of their family members who believed they were rushing things, they married in an empty church with Obinna's younger brother and Phoebe's only cousin as their witnesses. They had done it simply and noncelebratory but to Phoebe, it was enough to make it the happiest moment of her life.

*

Two days later, as they walked hand in hand back home on Obinna's last day in the village before returning back to work; the loud shrill cry of a woman around the thick bushes very close to her home stopped them. They rushed towards where the woman lay in the bushes bleeding profusely. She was a foreigner with ivory skin and pained hazel eyes. She was also heavily pregnant and by the looks of things, in prolonged labour. Why was she here especially in her, condition?

"Please save my child," she pleaded desperately, and Phoebe held her firmly already helping her through the process. Her late mother was a midwife and although she was not a professional, she knew the basics of childbirth. The woman was already crowning, and she needed to deliver this child safely. From the look of things, the woman was weak from blood loss. Meanwhile as for Obinna, the man rushed back home as quick as his legs could carry him to bring what she needed for this birth.

"I beg you; please do not let them have her. They drugged me and got me pregnant. For months, I have seen with my eyes the evil environment that... place is. I do not want my child to grow like that... I beg you," came out her desperate pleas. Phoebe encouraged her to save her strength for pushing. Obinna returned with towels, warm water in a flask, and one of her gowns for the woman to change into. After a gruelling hour of painful pushing, a beautiful baby girl with a lock of curly dark hair was born into the world.

"Oh my, she is the most beautiful child I have ever seen. Well done...," she told the woman who stared back at her and then suddenly her eyes gradually dimmed until there was no light in them. She had died still connected to her infant child. Phoebe held the crying infant and wept bitterly while Obinna held her in comfort.

Their mourning seized at the sound of bells and gongs approaching them. Phoebe had never seen the workers of the river temple because she steered clear of their occasional fetish displays during festivals, but nothing prepared her for their pronounced hedonistic representations. They were a mix of twelve youthful boys and girls dressed in white silk robes walking in three straight lines. Black and white paint adorned their faces, while their lips held palm fronds in them. In the front of the line was the sacred priestess of temple dressed in a white kaftan and red turban upon her head. She had a foreboding presence that Phoebe did not want to have anything to do with. At the sight of the dead woman, the workers began singing as though this was a thing of jubilation.

"Bless our goddess as the prophecy has come to pass. We welcome our vessel who found her way to her guardian," announced the priestess joining in the praises. Phoebe looked at Obinna who shook his head at her as if to say that confronting them would only lead to more problems.

"Quick, cut the umbilical cord and take the body of the carrier. Prepare it for a burial befitting of the one who birthed the vessel," commanded the priestess. At her command, four young men left the line and did as the priestess instructed.

Phoebe's silence was broken immediately, as she continued rocking the child whose cries seemed to intensify. It was obvious she was hungry. "This child's mother just died. She is not a thing that you refer to as 'it', how can you people be jubilant when a life was lost?" Obinna held her back from going to the priestess who turned to observe her.

"Ah, the guardian who does not know 'its' place," mocked the tall woman and then continued. "In the course of your role as a guardian, you shall learn swiftly that all which happens has already been predestined. Do you think that this woman just happened to locate your abode randomly a few days after we sent your summons through Okorie? Phoebe *Nkoli Nworie*...no...that has changed...it is now *Ejim*," revealed the priestess arrogantly showing her how informed she was of her life. "We have watched you as you matured until now. All that happened worked according to a process in which you would assume the role that has been in your family for centuries." Turning back to her underlings, the priestess commanded. "Bring the feedings for the infant." One girl brought forward a grey bag filled to the brim with baby food. "As long as you guide her, she will never lack in any way. You will treat her as you would your life; she will not have any markings on her body unless given by me, she will not feed on meat but fish, she must bathe every fortnightly from the spring of the sacred river, and she must never leave this village from now until when she assumes her role. Most importantly, this child must never offer her body or heart to any human man. As it is a celebratory occasion, I will leave you with wise words. Form no attachments with the vessel, failure to do so will incur dire consequences." The woman gave her a cold hard stare before turning her back to Phoebe. Without a second glance, the workers of the temple left as elusively as they had come.

If Phoebe was not carrying this child, she would not have believed that such a day had ever occurred.

7

Voices....

*H*ow long are you going to pretend that she has no obligations?" demanded the angry voice of the man Simdi always referred to as her uncle. He was her mother's older brother. He never seemed to like her, and Simdi did not know why. He visited her mother on some occasions, but these days his visits were beginning to leave behind sour aftertastes.

"You don't understand her as I do Okorie. How can you possibly expect me to treat her as if she was any less of a human being? I will never believe what they say she is, to me she is my daughter." Before she could continue any further, he cut her off angrily in a raised voice.

"Will you keep quiet?! Never over assume who you are to that thing, she is not as ordinary as we are. The minute you assumed your role as her guardian that unfortunate night, bad things have happened. Your husband mysteriously died one year after she entered your lives. What about me and how my two daughters

126

died because I reprimanded her? Before she came here, we were happy and prosperous, now no man wants you even though you are the prettiest woman they have ever come across in this village, and my wife has not had any more children. A curse hangs over us as long as she remains with us. Do not defend that *ogbanje*! I regret making that pact. I want you to return her to the temple. She has overstayed her welcome."

Simdi's heart clenched with sadness at the hatred laced in her uncle's voice. She waited for her mother to defend her but instead, her mother remained silent making her wonder if there was any truth in all her uncle accused her of? She had done none of the things she was accused of; she was sure. How could she possibly be responsible for the deaths of all those close to her? Simdi swallowed the disappointment suffocating her. What was she that made her uncle hate her so much? What was she that made people stay away from her? Who was she that could cause bad things to happen? Did her mother agree with him and would she soon be rejected because of these accusations? She remained silent even though she continued questioning herself.

"Get out!"

She was brought out of her musings by her *nne's* angry voice. This was the first time she was hearing such a tone from her mother towards uncle Okorie. It was her fault as well that her mother was shouting at her older brother whom she had confessed to Simdi was precious to her.

"What did you just say?" demanded Okorie in disbelief. "I said you should get out! How dare you say such rubbish about my daughter in my own house? If you cannot accept us, then you better leave this minute!" Her voice carried the finality of her decision.

Okorie being the proud man that he was stood and snarled at her *nne*. "She is not your daughter nor is she your child. You are a lonely widow and as long as that *thing* stays in this house, no man will ever be with you. The only one who was brave enough paid the price with his life, and any other stupid enough to be enticed by your beauty will die. Mark my words." Okorie left spitting outside to show how disgusted he was with his only sister as he left their house. She never saw him again.

Upon his departure, Simdi came out from where she had hidden; it initially was not her intention to eavesdrop but when she heard her name in the discussion, she became curious. Her legs shook as she approached her mother, who slumped on the chair tears rolling down her cheeks.

"*Nne*?" she called out. Her mother looked up at her as if she was staring right through her. When she finally spoke to her, it was with a hard-no-nonsense tone she always used in handling students in school.

"I will cut your hair; do you hear me? People will always talk about you, but you will not give them what to talk about, not anymore. Your hair is too long, it makes you stand out too much. It will be cut, and from now on you will have short hair like other girls. Do you hear me?"

Simdi nodded with tears in her eyes. She loved her long hair which fell to her shoulders, but it was always a subject of discussion wherever she went because of the soft springy texture so unlike every other person's hair in the village. People always talked about it and at that time, she was proud of how uniquely different it made her stand out. There would be nothing special about her anymore.

"Simdi...?" called out her mother questioningly but Simdi shook her head refusing to let the tears fall from her eyes.

"What am I mum? Why am I different?" She watched uncertainty pass her mother's eyes, but she did not provide an answer. It was years later, in the most unfathomable way that she would truly comprehend what she truly was.

*

The dog's insistent barking broke the spell of reminiscing that her memory cast on her. She sighed scratching her chin as she wondered what was prompting this behaviour from the dog. When she turned around, she saw a stone-faced Dalu approaching her. She wondered what she had done this time to evoke this expression from him. They were cordial with each other after their emotional session the other night and she did not have the strength to quarrel with him anymore. She also noticed he was starting to look better; he now held his messy dreadlocks in a loose ponytail, while his hands were always clean with well-trimmed nails. To top it all up, he wore the clothes she had washed for him. However, although he was making a conscious effort, she could still see that he rarely bath; and his beard looked too unkempt to be acceptable. She thought of neutral ways to suggest a complete adaptation of a cleaner appearance without starting another silent war with him. She gave him a wary look the moment he stood outside the kitchen door, which he returned with an expressionless one.

"Go inside..." he told her his voice sounding so final. Inside meant her room which was just absurd because she was cooking their evening meal. "I just began cooking, why should I...?" The look he gave her was a warning, one that made her keep quiet immediately. She put out the fire and walked past him, an uneasy feeling suddenly apparent as he followed her looking around.

"You are to remain in your room, please. Do not leave and stay out of the visible side of your curtain. Simdi, do I have your word that you will cooperate?" he asked and instead of answering, she ignored him in favour of walking into her room. Not long after he left, she heard voices outside, but she kept quiet wanting to know what was happening. She could not see who it was, but she knew it was a man. Judging from the greeting Dalu gave, she guessed this visitor was an older man. She could not help but hear the obvious hostility in his tone. The Dalu she interacted with since she came here was everything but hostile. He was brash, blunt, straight to the point, and sometimes even confrontational but he never resorted to hostility when he could simply ignore the matter altogether. She remained attentive as the footsteps moved from outside on to the living room where she could now hear them clearly.

"You are my son-in-law regardless of what has happened. Tomorrow we will be going to the church to pray for Kaima's soul and that of your sons. I am extending the invitation to you."

Even from where she sat Simdi could hear the reluctance in the man's voice. She silently thought back to some of the things Dalu had revealed to her. She did not know that his children, were dead. She assumed that he was a widower and his children were with relatives. It explained a lot of things about why Dalu was so reclusive and evasive to change; he was grief-stricken. It was possible that the loss of his family was enough to change him to what she was seeing now. It would not be presumptuous to believe that Dalu built this very house with the hope of spending the rest of his life with his wife and sons, but death had snatched them away. This thought saddened her; she was beginning to gain insight into Dalu's life.

Now attuned to Dalu, Simdi could identify the different variations of his silence and their meaning.

The silence accompanied with huffing sounds meant that he was embarrassed; the silence where he cleared his throat afterwards meant that he wanted to apologize; the silence that was truly silent meant that he was deeply thinking. She never worried when she witnessed those types of silence from his end. However, the most worrisome silence was the one where laughter followed after. It was never a good sign. It meant he was so angry that he was controlling its intensity with laughter. This was what was happening at the moment.

He began laughing even though it sounded flat and obviously false, "Ah *Akajiego* you ...came here..." more laughter "And... invited me to my own wife's... memorial service." He sounded like he was muffling his outburst with his palm but then he spoke again in a dead monotone. "I guess I should feel honoured that the richest in Umi is inviting me to a party. Hahaha ...a memorial service..."

The man cut him off indignantly, "You dare mock me after my consideration." At this point, Simdi was holding her anger at the man's arrogance. She did not know the relationship Dalu had with his father-in-law, but it was obvious that there was bad blood spilled between them.

"I will dare!" shouted Dalu startling Simdi and even his father-in-law. "Kaima was abused and neglected; she suffered greatly in the hands of your second wife while you stood there obviously uninterested in what happened to her. When I met your daughter, she was on the brink of giving up. I am not as wealthy as you are, but do you know what I offered Kaima that you could not? I gave her love. So much love that she was willing to sacrifice her position as your *Ada*, and the comfort of finer things for a nobody like me. I loved Kaima until there was nothing else that could compare to it. What did you give her?" When the man remained silent Dalu chuckled darkly, "you cannot even answer."

She wished she could see the other man's face. Was he remorseful or was he still blinded by prideful anger? "I will not deny that I neglected my daughter, but I want to do the right thing by inviting you..."
When Dalu spoke this time, he allowed his disapproval to spill out in his words. "Right? Do you even know what that word means Akajiego? Why the sudden need for you to do something right? When Kaima begged you to let her marry me, why did you ignore doing what was right?? You turned her away because all you could see was my *osu* label. You could never accept the child of an orphaned outcast as your son-in-law. You forgot how you begged my father to save Kaima's mother when she was gravely ill. Why did you

not reject his services since you already knew he was married to an *osu*? It does not matter that I was deemed unworthy by your biased standard but my Kaima... did not deserve the life she lived. Do you know that up until she died, her greatest regret was that not once did you see the children she bore? What changed that you decided to do something 'right'?" demanded Dalu who was now borderline furious.

"Your accusations are not needed I am..." the man shouted angrily but Dalu was unfazed.

"Ahh, now I see it. Your favoured second wife is dead, and you want to be free of your guilt since there is no one to assure you of the correctness of your neglect? Kaima... did not deserve the misfortune you as a father subjected her to," he declared so angrily and loudly that Simdi feared that a fight would soon ensue. This time the silence that descended on the room was stagnant. Dalu had finally hit the metaphorical hammer on the nail so much that it raptured. Simdi watched from the window as the man staggered dazedly out of the house. He opened his car and sat down inside staring at nowhere in particular. For a moment she pitied him; the death of one's child or parent was sad and not even comprehensible. Eventually, he drove off looking so wrecked that Simdi almost felt sorry for him.

Life was not always fair, people were cruel, and fate was tricky. All she wanted was to go and comfort Dalu, but she remained quiet. He may have comforted her when she needed it but knowing him, he would not want anything to do with her. Remembering her abandoned cooking, she left the room and heard the sound of wood being chopped. She noticed that the dog too which was normally active remained in a corner with its head inside its paws. The atmosphere was suddenly melancholy. She entered into the kitchen preferring to distract herself.

***

8 Years Ago.

It was New Year's Eve and every youth gathered under the moonlight as they partook in the festival of the last day of the year. It was a merry night with food, drinks, and entertainment courtesy of the king of Umi. This was an opportunity to interact with the peerage; young boys wooed girls and young girls enticed men. The local musicians beat their drums and sang in melodious songs. Dalu sat far away from the crowd, drinking and feasting quietly. Some girls blushingly looked his way and he returned their shy glances with foxy grins or mischievous winks. They were never confident enough to approach him, but he knew he was the challenge they yearned to explore even if it was just a simple tumble inside the bushes. He was the dirty secret that they wanted to have. Dalu never gave himself to any of them; he had lovers occasionally, but none was from Umi. They had taken everything from him, he would not feed their curiosity or let them taste the extent of his passion.

After an hour, a crowd gathered in a circle as they watched a dance competition between two girls. Curiously he walked to the crowd and was surprised when he saw Kaima dancing against another girl. She looked glorious as she displayed uninhabited dance moves. Everyone watched her, entranced by the graceful way she swayed her hips and the carefree abandonment to which she swung her arms.

All the girls were jealous of her and the attention she received that night. It was clear who would be the winner out of the pair. Her eyes landed on him and she gave him an inviting smile before continuing to match the beating of the drums with her dance steps. In that dark corner where he stood, he too admired her. Whereas others watched her merely captivated by the physical elements of her beauty and her dazzling smiles, he was spellbound by the internal strength that drove her. No one could tell that she was suffering, because she hid it so well.

Dancing in the moonlight was all a ploy that only he saw through; he could see the tears in the corner of her eyes as she twirled to the fast-paced music. Their friendship had grown stronger and Dalu out of consideration for Kaima's reputation tried all he could to prevent people from finding out that they met in the forest on each night of a full moon. If they found out that she snuck out to meet him, such gossip would ruin her. There was something between them; an unnamed thing that was present each time they saw themselves. It was firmly rooted in their ability to sense each other's presence, and the easy understanding that existed between them. It was in the way his heart throbbed when their fingers touched, and his almost desperate need to be close to her at the slightest excuse. He knew it was not infatuation, he wanted to be a part of her life, long term. She was the only one out of all the girls in Umi that he wanted to share himself with, but he held back because of the fear that he was not good enough for her. It was that fear that allowed him to look away each time she looked at his lips longingly; it was for the best.

His attention to Kaima returned when he saw one of the young men named *Ugo* walking towards Kaima. Ugo was the nephew of the king, a confirmed legitimate bachelor. Every girl wanted him; he was rich, handsome, and he knew all this. He was the type of person who would not be ashamed to walk up to Kaima because he was the kind of man who Kaima deserved. Dalu looked away jealously at the sight of them talking. He decided that it was time he went home. He had never been more *aware* than tonight that he did not belong here with any of them.

*

It was a very warm evening today and Dalu came to the forest to swim. Most mornings and afternoons, a lot of young people like him occupied the stream swimming, gossiping, joking around, and relaxing. He refrained from coming here at those times because they always asked him to leave. He was twenty years old now; he no longer possessed the zeal to engage in brawls. It further incited them that he gave no relevance to their opinion of him. He had come to terms with the fact that he was an outcast. Even though he lived in Umi because of his father's blood that flowed through his veins and the introduction of Christianity, his peers and the rest of Umi never allowed him to forget. So many times, he tried to understand their hatred for him, and the only explanation was jealousy. It never made sense to him because he was an orphan, and he was not rich. Why would people be so jealous of him? Even though he swore that the discrimination against him would not affect him, he did not have the tolerance this evening for confrontations by callous boys who saw him as a threat to their love interests and tried to provoke him to fight with them as a way of proving their masculinity.

As he entered the water, the coolness chilled his sweaty body instantly relaxing him. He enjoyed moments like this when he could be alone with his thoughts. The water always had a way of calming him. His late mother joked about how he stopped crying whenever she bathed him. Memories of his childhood were sweet glimpses that reminded him of his parents who did their best to give him a normal life. Being born into his family, he never felt the hatred of the people because his parents protected him with their love and devotion. They created a safe and loving environment in his life that lacked the villagers' disapproval. Even though things had ended tragically for them, he would never trade those memories for the world.

Remembering the events in his childhood, he was not blind to the scorn directed at his mother each time they walked side by side to visit Nwakaego. At that time, he never understood why his mother trekked a long distance into the market to Nwakaego's shop before she could buy the same foodstuffs near the shops close to his home. At the thought of his mother he sank deeper into the water, she always brought tears to his eyes. His mother had been a paragon of beauty; always radiant and welcoming. Her beauty which was so great that men left their wives in a bid to win her even though she was an osu; inevitably led to his father's death. He was being unfair to her memory but a part of his mind still heavy with grief always wondered if their lives would have been different if she had been an average looking woman.

He remained inside the river until sundown before deciding that it was time to leave. As daring as he was, he knew that it was not advisable to stay out in Umi for later than usual. Witches roamed the village, and not only them but other supernatural creatures that he was not in any way ready to confront. He came out wearing his discarded trouser which he was already outgrowing and made a mental note to visit Nwakaego's tailor before the next full moon. As he left the stream, he heard sobbing sounds coming from nearby. He was able to recognize the owner after a few seconds of listening; it was Kaima. He wondered why she was here at this time; it was not yet the full moon when they met. The last time he saw her, his jealousy had driven him away and since then they did not see each other. He was avoiding her until he was certain that he would not overreact if she suddenly announced that she accepted Ugo's advances. He found her crying on the top of a larger boulder close by, with her back turned to him.

"Kaima..." he called out softly and she almost fell off due to the surprise from his unexpected presence, but he was close enough to catch her.

"Take it easy," he whispered, and she relaxed immediately recognizing his voice.

Both of them were something, he thought slightly amused. They always met in the most deserted hidden places. Most times it was unplanned, but he was convinced that the universe was working hard to keep them apart from the rest of the world. Somehow it seemed improper because people would never understand their strange relationship.

People would misinterpret their meetings for a frolic in the forest. He hoped it would never come to that because Kaima deserved so much better than to live a life of ridicule. He studied her tear-stained face, noticing that she looked leaner than usual. Her figure was still intact but being as observant as he was, he could see that she was sick. Lines of fatigue marred her pretty face, and she had blisters around her mouth. Asides from the visible sickness it seemed that Kaima was losing that emotional battle she fought alone always. He feared that if one day he did not intervene, he would yet again lose someone precious to him. It was a sad thing to witness, it made him angry and uncharacteristically protective of her. He would not let her reach that point where her light finally disappeared.

"Why are you out here this late and not to mention crying?" he demanded not bothering to be subtle. He was a straightforward person and seeing her cry only infuriated him against the person who hurt her.

"Do I now need permission from you to cry?" she lashed out in a haughty tone pushing him away.

It dawned on him that he was encroaching on her privacy, but he decided he still wanted to know what made her cry at such an hour.

"Kaima what is it?" he asked again this time conscious enough to be gentle. He moved to stand in front of her finally seeing the swollen left eye. He wondered why he did not notice it at first when he observed her face. It was probably due to the shadows, which the early night cast on her or that she had strategically hidden her face. The anger that had been forming in his chest erupted, and he was now a raging volcano.

"WHO did this?" he shouted unable to control his astonishment. He saw her flinch even as she tried to hide her face, "it is not your concern Dalu leave me alone."

Dalu looked her in disbelief, "you who came to the forest asking for my friendship, now wants to be left alone? It is not possible because I have offered something I cannot take back. Now tell me who did this to you...?"

Kaima's eyes welled up with tears, "please, just let this be... don't make it worse.... just ignore it."

He would have let it go; he was someone who obeyed requests. However, the fear that dripped from her voice only fuelled his need to challenge the person that evoked such dread in her. He grabbed her shoulder and even though he was gentle, she screamed in pain. He stilled in his movements as his eyes carefully assessed her and without thought for propriety, Dalu unzipped her blouse to be graced with swollen red strips from her shoulder down to her back. No wonder she had screamed, no one deserved this sort of treatment. He was sure that this would leave a scar or two. Who had dared to inflict such brutality on an innocent girl like Kaima?

"How dare you undress me!!" she demanded angrily rushing to cover her back. When he remained frozen because of the unimaginable sight before him, she continued shakily. "Please say something... your silence makes me feel disgusting," she whispered crying unexpectedly.

He immediately came to her entwining their fingers and looking at her with a murderous expression. "Tell me who did it...was it your father?" When she frantically shook her head, his mind finally solved the puzzle, "I see." He released her and looked away as he drew in a harsh breath. How could a woman who had given birth to children, do this to another woman's child?

Dalu turned back to her clenching his fingers, "Listen to me Kaima, you will get up and you will follow me. We will see this matter settled now and not later. You are not a slave Kaima, neither are you a servant. You are the daughter of a rich man and today you will make that clear. If you do not get up right now, this very moment I will forcefully carry you." His voice rose higher than he intended, but it achieved its purpose because Kaima immediately nodded as she tried to zip her blouse, which he eventually helped her with. They left the forest holding hands; neither said a word because they knew that whatever was about to happen would not be easy.

*

Unlike the majority of people in Umi who lived in mud houses, Kaima's house was made from solid concrete bricks. It was a shining beacon that symbolized the extent of wealth that Kaima's father controlled. Only the wealthy traders or businessmen could build such houses, and it annoyed him even more that a *rich man's* daughter could be treated like a common housemaid. The compound was a big one surrounded by livestock leisurely moving around it. A large black and white bungalow stood in the centre with a mango tree behind it. Domestic workers were busy tending to their chores. When they saw them, one immediately went inside to alert the mistress of the house.

A little while later, Kaima's stepmother *Nkechi* emerged sending the servants indoor as she focused dark eyes on Kaima. "Useless girl.... Where have you been? Who do you expect to do your chores? Come here at once?" she commanded tapping her feet impatiently. Kaima made to obey, but he still had their hands held together and stopped her from moving.

"*Osu a*.... What do you want here? Get out!!!!!!" she ordered angrily while approaching them menacingly.

She was a fat woman with a big waist; it did not help that she was not too tall. However, Nkechi was a beautiful woman that any old-fashioned man would want as a wife. Underneath that smooth oval face and soft features was a wicked cruel woman.

Dalu calmly observed her not the least bit intimidated. "I am not afraid of you. I have met worse people; I just want to know why you hate Kaima so much. Why do you maltreat her so? What joy do you derive from constantly abusing her?" he demanded pointing at the swollen eyes and the broken disposition in Kaima's appearance and character.

"So, you went to report me to this *ekenswu*. You cheap harlot, has your standards sunk so low that you now consort with even an *osu?* I am not surprised, after all, you are just like your late mother; a prostitute that was punished with a shameful death."

He saw Kaima's eyes well up at the insult, and he squeezed her hands gently shaking his head. Today was the day she would finally stand up for herself, "this is not the time to cry. Do not let her talk you down or insult your late mother's memory like that." He intended for his whispered words to offer her assurance.

In that precise moment following his words, Kaima raised her head, squared her shoulders and surprised them all when she released their entwined fingers to administer a resounding slap across her stepmother's cheeks. "My mother was not a prostitute. She was ten times more of a woman than you would ever be." There was no fear in her eyes, as she looked straight into her stepmother's eyes fearlessly.

Nkechi's eyes widened in shock still holding her stinging cheek. In all her life she would have never predicted that Kaima would stand up to her in such a monumental way. She attempted to strike Kaima back but was rebuffed, because Dalu held it and applied enough force to hurt her.

"Never again will you dare touch her. She is not a slave, but the first daughter of a rich man. She is the *ADA* of this house, you, on the other hand, are a foreigner who was married into this house to reap what you did not sow," he retorted angrily as he released her hand.

The realization of what he said must have truly gotten across to her because her eyes widened affrontingly, and after a few minutes of silence Nkechi finally spoke with a venomous tone that mirrored her vehemence for being so humiliated. "Wait here .... You dared to strike me?!" she exclaimed as she left and entered the house.

When she came back, she was in tow with her oldest son *Tochi* who was six years old. He held a broom while his mother held a small bag of clothes. She threw the bag at Kaima, "get out of this place. No prostitute is allowed here. This is my husband's house. You are of no use to your father, just a useless reminder of the shameless woman he married. Get out!!!" Her words were meant to deliver the final blow that would destroy all Kaima's memories of her late mother, but Dalu refused to let the woman win.

"One day we will all die," he said to her calmly. "I pray you remember today as you did all you could to tarnish the image of a deceased woman while your young son watched on. When the time comes, what will he say of you?" he asked rhetorically knowing that he won when he saw her flinch, but he ignored her and instead went and picked Kaima's bag. He saw the indecisive look on Kaima's face. She looked as though she was confused at whether to stay and beg or to just leave with Dalu. "Let us go. I have a house far better than here, where you will stay away from this wicked woman. Nwakaego will love you and take care of you like she would her own child. Anywhere is better than here Kaima." Dalu offered pleadingly; he would not bear it if she chose to remain. Her stepmother might kill her. He was relieved when she nodded and let him lead her out of the house. Nkechi taunted them as they left, sweeping away their footsteps from the house as a way of saying they were bad fortune she was getting rid of.

As he led Kaima away from the place that was once her home, she broke down crying hysterically. Dalu consoled her making her a promise that day.
"If what you fear is your virtue and what would be said because you live with me, then you have nothing to worry about. I am a man of my words; I promise that I will protect you as long as I live.... I promise," he whispered to her wiping the tears from her eyes. As little as his words were, they seemed to reach her. When she finally looked at him with her tear-filled eyes, there was a silent agreement between them. She would trust him as long as he continued to protect her.

***

Hurt came in different forms and Dalu's own hurt came from the deep shattering feeling of lost love. It took and took from him until nothing remained. He wept for his late wife Kaima. He knew that secretly she always hoped that her departure from her father's home would push the man to finally love her. Her hope that he came back looking for her was never fulfilled while she was alive. Akajiego's lack of acknowledgement for her would forever remain one of the most hurtful things he did to Kaima. Her father's silence broke her. Dalu did not enter the house that night, rather he lay on the floor of his workshop replaying that fateful night that he arrived in toll with Kaima to Nwakaego's home. No one protested against his decision to liberate Kaima, but he saw the unvoiced worry in *Nne nwa's* eyes. Had she foreseen the harrowing hardship that awaited them?

*

Simdi was awoken by voices again in their small house. It was no longer the angry voice of uncle Okorie, this time it belonged to more than one person. A woman's voice accompanied by two men's deep voices, with that of her *nne*. She was alarmed because she could recognize the fear in her *nne's* voice. She quickly rose from her bed and crept towards the back of the door where she hid. She could not see them, but she could hear them clearly.

"We, the messengers of the river priestess, demand to know where you have hidden the vessel!" asked the woman reproachfully. Simdi blinked confusedly, vessel? Who could that be?

She held her breath as she listened closely to her mother's response, "oh great servants of the river I plead with you that you return another day for her. She is not here, she...." It dawned on her that her mother was lying. It made her worry even more because she never lied. For her to do so now meant that it was a dire situation.

Sensing the hostility emanating from the visitors, and without understanding why, she left the door and crawled away into the washroom. She was grateful that the door had been opened earlier when she woke up to ease herself, so she easily entered without being detected. Instinctively, she opened the black water barrel used to store clean water and without thinking she slipped inside it ignoring the coolness of the water that covered half of her. She shifted back the lid to carefully cover the barrel. Inside the dark container, Simdi waited for what seemed like the longest minutes of her life even as she began shivering from the cold water. Her decision to hide was tested finally when sounds of struggle could be heard and then the voices drew closer to the opened bathroom door.

"Did I not say that she is not here? If she was, what would I possibly gain by withholding her?" demanded her *nne* indignantly, "she went to her friend's home and remained because of the heavy rain."

There were so many questions that Simdi wanted to ask and she prayed that she survived this night to ask them. From where she hid, she heard glasses being broken, things inside their room being rummaged and upturned, but Simdi kept quiet pleading silently that her *nne* would not be hurt because of her. It seemed to take forever but then silence returned inside the room. Her heartbeat accelerated when she heard footsteps approaching the container; this was it. She stilled instinctively, waiting in anticipation. Time passed, and suddenly the lid slowly began to open. To her surprise when she looked up, rather than the face of danger, she saw her mother's fear-stricken face looking down at her. Gradually her mother's fear was replaced by relief and the next thing Simdi knew, she was pulled up and encompassed in her mother's loving hug.

"You remembered," muttered her mother amidst sobs. Her mother quickly brought a towel and began towelling her. "I'm so sorry. I won't let them take you. I promise," she whispered with fingers that trembled more than Simdi, who shivered from the cold.

As she sat there on the floor being towelled dry by her mother, a sudden memory that explained the sudden compulsion to enter the water barrel surfaced. It was a year ago on the night of her fifteenth birthday when bad people came to their home and her mother had hidden her safely inside the container. Even then, those people had wanted the same thing; they had wanted to steal the vessel...

"What is this vessel mother? Why do those people want it so desperately?" she asked suddenly overcome with apprehension over the answer she would receive. Instead of a reply, her *nne* pulled her again into a tight hug and looked deep into her eyes.

"I will protect you. I swear that I will," declared her *nne* refusing to let go of her. Simdi nodded truly believing her *nne*. No matter what, her *nne* would protect her.

8

Sadness....

The minute Simdi woke up, a deep sense of sadness overtook her. She closed her eyes trying not to feel it, but it refused to go away. It remained close to her like a quiet observer who would forever be present as long as she existed. She sat up ignoring the pounding of her head as her mind recalled what she dreamt of. That night served as an eye opener to her circumstances. It was depressing remembering the heights that her mother reached to set her free from her ties to the river. Ultimately, their rebellion welcomed a host of other troubles for them. She sat up and sighed tiredly; there was no use remembering the past? Stretching languidly, she noted that she overslept.

As she walked outside the house, she realised that it was too quiet. From the dishevelled pile of wood and an ajar door leading into Dalu's workshop, she predicted Dalu did not sleep in the house yesterday. She had waited almost all night to hear his footsteps to no avail. She understood what today was after all; yesterday's visitor had revealed it. Simdi was still at a loss on what to do because more than ever, the man in question would not want her sympathy. His avoidance and silence further intensified how sombre the day would be. The clap of thunder brought her out of her deep thoughts and as she looked up towards the sky, she thought of how ironic it would be if it rained today of all days. She spent the better half of the hour searching for him and when she could not find him, her panic grew. If it were any other day Simdi would not have been so worried but today especially, was the anniversary of the woman he felt deeply for. Who knew what he would do? She silently prayed that he would not do anything callous. She could be overreacting; there was a possibility that he had gone off to sell his sculptures or to the market to buy food. Eventually Simdi pulled out a stool and sat in front of the house; she would wait for him.

*

"Dalu... I think my feet will need constant night rubs again."

They were in their bedroom cuddled up together that night. The children had long gone to bed after exhausting themselves from their school lessons. Just looking at his wife's face that radiated with happiness was enough for Dalu to deduce what was going on. "Wait, what? Kaima... you are with child?" Kaima's smile confirmed it and he just stared in shock. After they had their second son, they agreed that they would not have any more children until things got better for them. It did...

"Remember that we said... we would have a daughter in our own home and things have gotten better so far. Last year we moved from Nwakaego's house and into the home of our dreams. This beautiful place that you built just for us...I stopped preventing the pregnancies Dalu. I'm ready to have more children. Our dream to have a large family... why put it off? Are you not happy?" she asked suddenly worried that he did not want this pregnancy.

Dalu wanted a large family, he always did because he was constantly reminded of the loneliness of living as an only child. It was his dream to have a family filled with children who would grow in love and friendship. Part of the reason he suggested not having any more children was because of her health, they had been advised against having more children. Even though things were going fine for them now that his sculptures were nationally recognized in more than twenty communities, he did not want to risk her health.

"Ima, you know that I am happy that we will have a child... it is just that ... I am worried because the last two pregnancies were not easy. I am scared for you my love." He closed his eyes not wanting to see her disappointment at his lack of enthusiasm.

He felt her warm fingers trail a path down his eyes, "it's been four years since my last birth. What could possibly go wrong?" She asked him so confidently.

*

Thinking back now to that moment Dalu decided that they were foolish to have blindly walked into the trap that Fate had set for them.

It did not matter how many times he visited Kaima's grave, the feeling of loss and sadness always felt the same. His shirt was long discarded somewhere along the way here. Today marked the sixth year of his wife's death. He buried her close to the home of their dreams. Nwakaego and her son came that day to pay their last respects. He remembered the anguish he felt as he and *Chinedu* placed her coffin into the cold ground. With his hands he had made her casket, and with those same hands and sheer will he had dug her grave. What could go wrong? Kaima had asked months before the delivery of their stillborn child; it

158

was a prolonged labour that ended in death. His precious Kaima who could not hurt a fly had died. He did not understand why fate would take away his wife who had loved him without shame. It happened so quickly that he had been unable to even tell his sons about the demise of their mother. It was Nwakaego who had done that for him while he was grief-stricken; she held them gently and explained that their mother was never coming back.

Everything went downhill from then onwards. How was he supposed to know that a week after, they too would perish? Nothing remained the same after his wife's death, but Dalu tried his best to comfort his children. The next few days without sleep, he cared for his sons. He fed them, played with them even when they were reluctant, and assured them that their mother was alright where she was. On the day they died, he was so tired from lack of sleep. He just closed his eyes for a few minutes inside his workshop and was awoken by the screams of his son Oyiri. In panic, he dashed out only to see Ifeanyi slumped down with his throat swollen, while blood sipped from his lips and lifeless eyes. In their palms, they clutched onto red poisonous wild berries.

"Oyiri... no ... Ifeanyi ... nooo."

Wasting no time, he hefted them on his shoulders and ran madly into the village seeking help. That was the biggest mistake of his life because no solution was found. Instead, he was shunned and almost killed. Later when he returned their bloated bodies to the home, he washed them, cloth them, and buried them beside their mother's grave.

Dalu blinked from the memories, as he stood still in front of his wife's grave which he hardly visited. He chose to be the coward who for so long avoided her grave to escape the painful events of their past. It made him face the realities of the day he had been hit with the shock of her death. Some days when he visited, he would blame her at first for the grief, and then he would blame her innocent soul for leaving him. He called her cruel, and then blamed her some more. When their sons died, he had blamed her even then. It was all her fault; she left him, their functional family and the bonds they had formed in their new life together. He called her weak, wicked, and when he was out of words to call her, he blamed her even more. Later on, as the days continued counting until she was just a fragment of his memories, he realized that he was the one who had truly been at fault. He should have never gotten her pregnant even when she had a hand in it. He should have never slept at all when his children were unattended to, because those few moments of slumber were what had killed his children.

He lay beside her grave, as the sun caressed his skin. For a while it was warm then slowly it became scorching. "Kaima," he whispered not knowing what else to say to the woman that had once been his.

*

It was evening when Simdi finally saw him. All day she had been worried and scared that he would finally give in to the grief because of the pain he still felt. Sadness had the power to crack even the toughest of men. She had been in that situation before and she could relate to it.

Since yesterday, she constantly questioned her decision to remain here with Dalu. She did not want to cause him pain as she caused everyone who helped her. When she fled from the *river village,* she met some people who she took refuge with. After a month of bliss, one night something bad happened. The kind man who allowed his wife to take her in, returned from the stream after fishing only to slump and die. She knew it was her that brought about the death of the man, even though no one pointed a finger at her; she was sure she caused it. She left before she could do any of them more harm. She walked for days and nights, hungry and sick with no hope of resting. It was in a moment of weakness that she decided she wanted to die. She knew that it was cowardly, but she was alone, tired, and without any form of hope. As she sat in despair studying the poisonous leaves she plucked, she kept telling herself that it was for the best. Just a moment before she could do any harm to herself, something like an epiphany assaulted her with images of the night her mother held unto her desperately with her last breath. The things she told her and the thought of how her mother risked her life to save her was enough to make her stop her rubbish attempt at suicide; she did not want her mother's death to be in vain.

Her thoughts were brought back to the present when she heard the dog barking and on looking ahead, she saw Dalu walking into the compound. She was at a loss of what to say to him, but relief washed over her knowing he was fine. He was dirtier than he had ever been since she saw him. There was mud on his body and clothes, and it covered his hair as well. It must have been because of the rain; did he lay on the bare ground during such heavy rain? He did not acknowledge her, choosing to walk past her as he entered into his room. Simdi remained outside watching the light drizzle that the rain changed into.

She wanted to leave him to his privacy although it would be only today.

A few minutes must have passed when she saw him walking back towards her with a stool which he set a few meters away from her. He had cleaned out the mud on him and changed his clothes, but his hair was still spotting some patches of mud which she decided not to comment on. He came back with two cups and one bottle of whiskey. They did not speak when he sat down or when he poured her a cup and handed it to her.

"You didn't ask if I drink," she pointed out and he shrugged.

"Pour it to the earth if you do not then," was his dismissive reply.

She looked away deciding to be his drinking companion even though she had never tasted the alcohol in her whole life. Being who he was, he just did not know how to ask for her company, so she would do it without his permission. Between them, he was the difficult one no matter how well he hid it.

The minute the amber coloured liquid touched her lips, it sent a burning sensation down her throat. She coughed out uncomfortably trying to catch her breath. When she looked up again, dark eyes watched her with a flicker of interest.

"Is it your first taste of liquor?" he asked, and she blushed furiously.

"In my defence, I was focused on other things," she blurted out already ready to argue. He waved off her explanation with his long fingers.

"Please, never explain yourself to anyone. If you have waited until now to indulge, then treat it as it is. I only asked because it seemed like I wasted too much of good liquor on a non-drinker. I should have just given you a cap full." She was about to retort when she realised that he was joking with her. She kept quiet and stole glances at him. Why was he suddenly looking normal? He was acting like today was an ordinary day.

"If you have something to say, instead of looking at me like a lost lamb...just come out and say it," he told her and turned to her.

There were many things to say, but she was uncertain of how she would say them without offending him, "I know what today is to you. I'm just surprised that you seem normal" she admitted attempting to sip the drink again. It still burned, but she was beginning to notice the warmth that it provided as well.

"I have had six years to adjust to it," he said shoving his hands into his loose hair. "It is not that I am not sad. In fact, I want to go inside and crumble into an emotional wretch. Would it change what happened? Would it bring them back?" Brief silence passed between them before he offered her an apologetic smile despite himself, "I am sorry that I worried you."

Simdi blinked in surprise at the unexpected statement, "You shouldn't be... I thought..."

He chuckled but kept looking at the starless clouds, "that I would kill myself? No, although not from lack of trying. I always lose the mind to; I always question if this is how I meet my end after all I have been through? I have this one-sided competition with Fate. As stupid as this sounds, by living as horribly as I have all these years, I think it is my way of challenging any power observing."

She burst out laughing and after a while she stopped, "It's not funny," supplied Simdi awkwardly. "When he did not share in her humour, she cleared her throat and explained the reason for her mirth. "You ...sound like me. I sat somewhere a year ago and wanted nothing more than to die, but then I said the only punishment I could give to my destiny was to keep escaping with my life. It must have been valuable for my mother to pay such a high price." He did not reply even after what remained of that laughter were eyes shining with unshed tears.

Eventually, he turned to her and replied in such a soft voice, "It is valuable." Then he proceeded to gulp up all the content in his cup. He poured himself a second cup sighing. "We were children when we met, Kaima suffered all her life, and I gain some consolation in the belief that marrying me at least offered her a better life than she had in her teenage years. Her father was the richest man in the village. She should have lived a charmed life, but that woman suffered so much; thinking of it breaks my heart. I met her when she was this close to giving up," he revealed pinching his fingers. "We were so different, by now you know that I am an offspring of an osu; a quota of the society considered as *'things.'* In the eyes of the villagers, my kind is seen as disgusting abominations who should never associate with the esteemed ones. My father did not care, he saw my mother and the rest was history." A sad smile replaced the annoyed expression, "Kaima did not care too. She kept chasing after me even when I did not know. When she finally caught me, I did not stand a chance. She gave up everything for my sake. Ironically, it was the year after I prospered in my business that she died. Blood clot during her prolonged labour ... it still shocks me."

Simdi listened attentively absorbing every word that Dalu spoke. When he did not say anything again, she turned to see that his lips were trembling. "I...have never experienced anything except parental love...but I... believe that you loved her very much. It's why it hurts even after now. I ... don't think you should live your life forever blaming yourself for all that happened. You and I ...we all are humans. There was no way that you could predict all that would happen."

He scoffed and drank the second cup unfazed, she wondered if he was now so accustomed to the burning sensation from the alcohol that it no longer stung. "What then should I do if I do not live forever punishing myself...what?" he demanded weakly.

She set her unfinished drink near the window and turned to him, "Your wife sacrificed so much as you said to be with you right? When you were with her, did you not share the best moments of your life? What if that's what she wants? What if she wants you to continue living to the shame of all who think you are an abomination? Imagine if you turned from grief to joy; they would be defeated because you have withheld the satisfaction of them witnessing you existing miserably."

She took his silence as rebuff but then as she looked towards him, she saw him struggling with his emotions. The darkness helped shield his break down, but she could see how sad he truly was. They remained seated outside in silence but chose to stay by his side offering him a presence that would not interfere with him struggling so emotionally as tears rolled down his eyes. It continued to rain and Dalu silently continued to shed the tears he did not know was in there waiting to be set free.

9

Steps....

*S*he was sleeping soundly as Dalu laid her gently on the bed inside her room. It was typical that a girl as reserved as Simdi would be a lightweight when it came to alcohol. Looking at her now without her consciously shying away from his gaze; he discovered that Simdi was far more different than anyone he came ever across. The mystery surrounding her was obvious but somehow, he managed to do something significant enough to earn her trust and solidarity.

He was afraid of her, he realised because she was the type of woman who would hurt him without even knowing that she did. It had taken a few words from her to break his resolve. After he seized crying, to his greatest surprise when he turned to her, he was struck with startlingly understanding eyes that seemed to bear empathy towards his grief. In all the time that he lived after the death of his family, not once did he consider if the way he chose to live was the way that Kaima would want. She always told him that her wish for him was happiness. Each time they celebrated their anniversaries or birthdays, she never failed to remind him of that. He was tired he thought, as he entered into his lonely room plagued with memories of the last day he spent with his beloved wife.

*

"You will always be happy?" she pressed on kissing his fingers.

"When you are here with me, why not?" he replied smiling dotingly at her. He moved towards her and kissed her protruding stomach.

Kaima smiled at him kissing the top of his head. "You haven't answered me...," she pressed on.

He smiled pushing up to the bed and gathering her in his arms, "of course I will. I will always be happy with you."

She shook her head, "what of without me? What of if I am..."

He cut her off, offended by how carelessly she would ask such a question. "Why would you ask something so insensitive? How do you expect me to be happy without you? I would...," he stopped talking because the thought itself was unfathomable. Why would he live without Kaima? He would follow her instantly without a moment's hesitation; Kaima was his world. If she was not in it, he would have no purpose for living. Warm hands covered his chest where his heart was beating erratically at the thought of her not existing.

"Thank you Dalu for loving me so. Sometimes I wonder if I deserve to have a man so devotedly in awe of me but then again, I love you just as much, and I want you to know that I cannot wait to have this child."

"I love you too," he said without hesitation.

She smiled and looked into his eyes, "I will be the happiest woman in the world if you are always happy... no matter the situation we find ourselves. Promise me you will always be happy?"

He made that promise to her as she fell asleep with a blissful smile on her face. The next afternoon Kaima entered premature labour. She died along with the child that never stood a chance in the fight to live.

Simdi woke up feeling lightheaded and far too tired for someone who slept as long as she did. She remembered yesterday's events and cringed at the fact that she fell asleep when Dalu was still emotional as he had been. Looking around, she wondered how she woke up in her room. From what she remembered, she fell asleep with her head resting on the window. Was it possible that Dalu carried her back into her room? No that was not possible, she must have staggered inside here, right? Yawning tiredly, she stood up and took her toiletries with her. Usually Dalu would be out of his room by this time so she could take her bath. She was so relieved that her injuries from the snakebite and stabbing were all healed. As she towelled her body and was about to put on her dress, a wave of pain washed over her neck and she stumbled to the ground biting her lips until she tasted blood. This was a sensation she was familiar with, and she knew from experience how to hold in her screams. The pain concentrated on her neck seemed to go on forever while she took laboured breaths on the bathroom floor. It hurt so much, this branding that was part of her existence; it hurt always. Would she ever be free of this pain?

All at once as always, the pain left her completely and she crawled towards the standing mirror to examine herself. It was no surprise when she saw the appearance of a single thick black stripe of line wrapped around her neck symbolizing her bondage chain and unspoken slavery to the river goddess. In anger, she pushed the mirror aside ignoring the shattering sound the object made on impact with the hard floor. Her heart began pounding erratically; this was her fault. For a moment she had forgotten what she truly was because of the peace she felt living with Dalu.

She looked at her left upper arm anxiously and released a sigh of relief when she discovered that the four other black strips one inch apart from each other were not yet visible. Her head was spinning wildly, and she quickly wore her dress wrapping the towel around her neck. Without hesitation, she collected the largest piece from the broken mirror and ran out of Dalu's room. In her haste, she did not see him walking towards her and she crashed into the man. There was a brief moment when each of them stood still with her panting nervously while he appeared surprised from the abruptness of the collision. The moment was broken when he attempted to steady her, but she retreated instantly wearing an expression of a cornered cattle on its way to the slaughterhouse.

"No... don't ...please just leave me," she demanded pushing past him as she ran into her room.

The last thing that she wanted was for him to see her neck. She needed to break the already forming bond that the priestess was reconnecting within her. It had taken her and her mother almost two years to successfully fade the lines; at the cost of her mother's life. The goddess would never possess her even if it meant that she would lose her life as well.

***

Ten Years Ago

Her whole body hurt.

There were hands moving across her naked body intrusively as she lay still in the water. She was always scared whenever a fortnight drew near; it marked a scheduled time that they always came uninvited to take her to the river. They washed her in sweet smelling fragrance and covered her body in soft silk. When they were done, they gently combed her long hair that never stopped growing no matter how many times she cut it. After the bathing ritual was done, she was set in a kneeling position with her head bowed and her arms outstretched. She waited and waited as the silence became unbearable.

"Oh my, how fast you are growing. By the time you are twenty, you would have fully embodied the goddess," whispered a woman who trailed her fingers around her neck and down her upper arm. It was the same voice from all those years. The voice of the faceless woman who pierced her ears, who hit her when she asked too many questions, and who reminded her always that her stubbornness would result in harsher treatments. She was afraid of this woman.

Suddenly, the smell of incense filled the room as soft chants from the people surrounding her floated across the room. She did not fully comprehend it, but she knew that something wrong was happening. Dizziness overtook her and then something forcefully wrapped itself around her left upper arm. Fear replaced the surprise as pain washed over her arm. It felt like someone tied a rope around the spot and consistently dug into it with the intent of cutting off that arm. Simdi had never felt so terrified, she began shouting and begging for mercy. This was a pain she could not bear, and she could not understand why her mother would allow her to be subjected to such cruelty.

Simdi remained in her room for two days and each of Dalu's attempt at inquiring over the matter was rebuffed. Every day he would set a plate of food for her, but it repeatedly remained untouched. The only time he caught a glimpse of her was whenever she used the bathroom and even then, she refused to speak to him. Dalu could not understand what happened that day in the time-space of her bathing and the time it took for him to respond to the shattering sound inside the room. He had rushed from the living area where he was napping to see her running blindly out of his room. The expression on her face was bleak at first with her looking unfocused and then as though she awoke to her surroundings, it turned hunted. The expression was identical to the one she wore on the night they saw the witch. What happened to her inside the bathroom? Had she seen a ghost?

*

Something was not right. He felt it deep within his bones when he returned from his journey outside town. It was drizzling lightly outside, and his clothes were drenched by the time he entered inside the house. As he approached his room, he heard scraping sounds of the stool falling inside of Simdi's room. He dropped his work tools and rushed into the room to see her collapsed on the floor holding a jagged piece of the broken mirror from his bathroom. He was instantly horrified when he saw the blood dripping down her left arm from deep ugly self-inflicted cuts; she was barely conscious.

"No...no...," he practically shouted as he removed his shirt and tied her injured arm. "Why did you do this...Simdi why?" he demanded in frustration while lifting her unto the bed. The nearest hospital was twenty minutes away. If he carried her now, would they make it before she finally died of blood loss?

"Please listen to me...," begged Simdi breathing weakly as she gripped his shirt desperately.

He did not wait for her explanation, "just shut up. You do not get to tell me anything at this point," he angrily stated.

Simdi shook her head stubbornly, "I ...I...won't die...they will be ...gone before you...know it...please just believe it... I did this to buy more time. Do you...do...see anything around my neck?" she asked weakly.

She was not making sense but Dalu indulged her. "No...nothing" he relayed, and that answer caused her to smile shakily. "It worked... I ...just ...need water." It was barely audible but Dalu could hear the relief in her voice.

After he provided her with the water she requested, he carefully applied crushed herbal leaves on all the cuts on her arm. She was right; she would not die from these cuts because she was careful not to puncture any major vein. It made him wonder how exactly she knew where to cut herself without truly inflicting life-threatening injuries. How long had she become accustomed to such cruelty?

*

Cold brown eyes stared back at Simdi when she opened her eyes. Dalu made sure that she saw how unimpressed he was with what she did. How could she explain that for her to sever the links formed with the goddess, she had to inflict pain on herself as well as break all the rules her mother revealed to her. She knew she could trust him, but she was afraid that he would fear her if he knew what she stood for. She was the vessel that the goddess would eventually possess for her continued existence within the human realm. It took her mother years of careful experimenting to discover the extent of which the rules could be broken before she finally revealed the truth to Simdi. After that, they ran away from the river village where her mother continuously broke the rules to weaken the link.

"If you can sit up, then do so. You need to eat, or you will die." He made sure not to acknowledge her pleading eyes directed at him when he set the plate of food in front of her. She nodded before forcefully swallowing all the bread and chicken soup he prepared. She dared not point out that the taste was disgusting because of her morning breath. When she was done, he gave her water which she drank without hesitation.

"Dalu please..." she attempted when his silence was too much to bear.

"If you will not explain everything to me then please do not apologize," he told her collecting the plate and cup.

He attempted to walk out of the room, but he was unable to hold his words. Turning to her downcast face, he bit out, "you sat there that night and told me we were alike. It was you who declared that living was your goal. Yet you would harm yourself so unthinkingly..."

Simdi felt nauseous at his words but she stumbled out of bed and held onto his arm. "Do you think I would do that without having a reason? I ...whether you believe it or not, I did it so that I could buy myself more time here with...you Dalu." She sounded desperate, but she did not care. All she cared about was that this man believed her.

When he looked at her this time, he made sure that he looked straight into her hazel eyes. "What is it Simdi, what is it that made you so scared?"

Simdi opened her mouth, about to say it all when she lost all her courage, "I..."

He sighed sullenly and then gently released her hold on his arm. "Sleep or bath...please...just do not do anything like that again and be careful with your injured arm." With that said, he left her room.

Simdi slumped on the floor in frustration realising that this was no longer her fear of Dalu finding out the truth. It was her hesitation in revealing to someone else what had taken her mother twenty long years to reveal to her.

*

It was late afternoon, and already the sun was preparing to set. Due to the small rain yesterday, the atmosphere was very cold. Dalu sat on the wooden stool under the palm tree, as he separated two bowls of warm water which would be used to wash his dreadlocks. This particular activity brought back nostalgic memories of his childhood and rare moments spent with his late mother. Washing his hair had been one of the activities he looked forward to because it was their own opportunity to spend time together. His mother had been a beauty with smooth chocolate coloured skin, an oval face, striking light brown eyes, a straight cute nose, dimpled cheeks, and a beauty mole on top of the right side of her lush lips. She was the sunlight that attracted every single person who ever saw her; he had inherited this particular trait from her as well. He easily attracted people to him even when he did not want the attention. As an only child, he had been closest to his mother, who pampered him at any opportunity. Through her constant parables and stories, she instilled both cultural and moral roots within him.

"Dalu stop moving, you will get soap in your eyes," cautioned his mother to a younger twelve-year-old version of Dalu.

Dalu cheekily giggled and tried to shake off the foams, "But it tickles. I cannot hold my laughter or shaking," he complained mischievously.

His mother rinsed out his hair and then wrapped his hair and half of his face with a towel. "Mama, I cannot see!" he complained.

"Serves you right for getting my clothes wet," mocked his mother as she led him to the stool and began towelling his hair. "Your father will think I look ugly when he comes back." It was a joking remark she always made; it was no secret that her husband adored her.

Dalu pushed away the towel obscuring his face and looked at his mother appreciatively, "I do not think you can ever look anything but beautiful mama."

Dalu's reminiscing halted when he felt soft warm hands running gently through his scalp. He was kneeling close to water drainage outside the house with his back turned to everything else. For a moment, he entertained the thought that he was hallucinating about the image of his late mother. When he looked up, he saw that instead of his warm loving beautiful mother washing his hair, it was Simdi with her captivating eyes and startling beauty who stood above him spreading soapy lather all over his scalp. Some of it trailed down into his wide opened eyes and he winced at the stinging sensation.

"Please close your eyes... here sit down instead of kneeling," she instructed him bravely motioning towards the bench beside him; she knew she was encroaching heavily on his boundaries. It occurred to him that this was her way of reconciling with him; they had not spoken since that day. He sat down and bent his head towards the drainage while she began washing his dreadlocks filled with mud and accumulated dirt.

"You're so lucky that you don't have lice or dandruff," Simdi stated pouring more shampoo into his hair before she rigorously began scrubbing his scalp and locks. He closed his eyes enjoying the sensations that her masterful fingers sent all over his body; it was oddly therapeutic. Even if he was still annoyed with her, he had to admit that this was relaxing.

"My mother used to do this for me till I was...sixteen," he admitted despite himself. He felt her hands halt in his head; she was surprised that he was sharing a part of himself when she was tightly holding on to a secret. This was his way of extending an olive branch to her.

"I... my hair when long... was washed by my mother as well." It was whispered, but he heard it.

Despite his annoyance with her, he found himself opening up to her even further about his mother. "She was so beautiful Simdi; I remember that before I started sculpting, the first thing that I ever made for her were pretty sun-shaped earrings. She was so proud of it and she wore it everywhere even when she owned better jewellery. She showed it off to everyone and even my dad expressed how he was impressed at my creativity...so much that he bought me my first chisel... the thing is blunt now, but I still carry it everywhere." Warm water touched his scalp rinsing away the dirty foam.

"I ... can draw," she confessed shyly. "I started drawing so that I would not forget the things I saw whenever I could, I left my drawing book when I ran away, I'm sure it's destroyed but... my *nne* was proud too. I think our parents will always be proud of us no matter how simple or vast our talents are."

They were silent for a while before Dalu decided to speak as she rinsed his hair a second time, "I was ...more scared than angry a few days ago. Simdi..." he sighed and continued, "whatever it is, you can trust me with it." At his words, she went still in her ministrations on his head.

She left him and picked up the towel, which she placed around his hair and started rubbing it. "I do...it's just ..." she stopped talking and he let her.

Looking up at her from where she stood above him drying his hair, he reached for her injured arm. "I do not ever want you to hurt yourself. You should treat yourself kindlier," he pleaded softly as they continued to search each other's eyes.

Simdi gave him a wide-eyed expression as though she was seeing him for the first time before she proceeded to kiss him out of the blue. In his shock, he pulled away from her halting the chaste kiss immediately. She, on the other hand, looked dazed standing there with her hands grazing her lips. He saw when she realized what she had just done, because she moved away from him in embarrassment.

"I am sorry, I am so sorry," she whispered as she hurriedly dropped the towel on his laps and rushed back into the house.

Dalu sat there momentarily dazed before realisation gripped him; she was the first woman he was kissing in six years since Kaima died. Suddenly a deep sense of guilt at the thought of him betraying his wife's memory washed over him.

*

Upon entering her bedroom, Simdi proceeded to scold herself repeatedly for doing something so brashly stupid. What had possessed her to kiss Dalu? She had no right to do it, and yet she had stolen a kiss from him just when he stated that he cared about her. She went to the wall and tapped the back of her head on the surface. He did not kiss her back but instead, he looked so shocked that the only thing she could do was to flee because she was ashamed of herself. It was just that looking at Dalu from where he sat with his open expression and comforting words, had misled her. It was the first time a man was looking at her as though she was the most precious thing on earth. The fact that he was transforming right before her eyes did nothing but encourage her further to test her growing feelings for him.

He was changing from the recluse into a person more appealing and alluring. Without the dirt concealing with his appearance, he was truly ruggedly handsome. Since they met, she simply focused on his other attributes such as his kindness, protectiveness towards her, and his generosity, but that close to him just a few seconds before she had kissed him; she realised that she wanted his intense brown eyes to always look at her. In that defining moment when her heart had pounded so loudly, Simdi decided to take a chance. If she was going to kiss any man for the first time, why not Dalu? She had meant it to show him she was entrusting herself into his care, but she knew she did it wrong. Dalu probably saw her as just one of those girls that were sure to hang off him if this was how he looked on a normal basis. What could she do to resolve this? With her own two hands, she had pushed them back to square one where they would awkwardly tolerate themselves.

***

Dalu could not concentrate.

His thoughts kept on chasing after the memory of the awkward kiss Simdi initiated. Her inexperience was obvious in the way she had only placed her lips on top of his. Could he even call what had happened a kiss? Maybe she meant to peck him and missed his cheeks...right?

He cleaned remnants of shaving cream off his neck after he had trimmed his beard to the desired density. Looking at himself in the mirror, he smiled. He looked so different from the man he had been six years ago.

Before him, stood someone weathered, mellow, and stained from life's experiences; a mixture of good and bad.

Remembering the brief kiss, he felt a sense of betrayal towards Kaima even when he knew he was long past feeling that way. It grew from the fact that he was starting to claim back the life he had once lived before the grief of losing his family possessed him. To him, he had no right to think of any other woman. Since her death, he had stayed celibate choosing to ignore all physical urges. They were suddenly reawakened, thanks to Simdi. He decided that for both their sakes, he would not acknowledge it. He was experienced enough to know the signs of hero worship; Simdi felt indebted to him. She did not really want him, and he was just the most convenient choice she had to feed her curiosity.

It hurt thinking of it that way, but it was the truth. He would hardly be a choice if Simdi lived a normal life. A girl as beautiful as her would have ended up with someone far more acceptable than he. As he left his room, he wondered how in the world he would rid himself of the memory of how soft her lips felt against his.

*

It was evening when Simdi left her room after partaking in bouts of self-shame. She knew she had to face Dalu eventually. Therefore, she braved up and reluctantly walked out of her room to the kitchen. It was getting to the time when she was supposed to prepare dinner; worrying would not feed her or Dalu. She halted when the aroma of food ambushed her and when she walked into the dining area, she saw that the table was already set.

"Simdi? I was going to call you just now...," came Dalu's voice from the back door that connected to the kitchen. This reminded her of the time before her birthday when she had surprised Dalu with a good meal after they quarrelled. Was this how out of place he had felt then?

Simdi was sure that she was making a face; the man in front of her was Dalu but at the same time, it was not him.

"Uhm did you do something with your hair?" she asked stupidly, and he laughed handing her a cup before taking his seat at the head of the table.

"I just trimmed the tips that were too chunky. Does it look bad?" he asked his hands skimming through his locks self-consciously.

Simdi sat down too and tapped her forehead. "It... it's a nice look and the beard..." she stopped.

How in the world did he expect her to look at him when he looked like this? Was this why he never bothered to look good, because he looked too good? She was not making sense; Dalu was dazzling to look at with his long thin dreadlocks left to fall over his shoulder. She had always known what he looked like but tonight with his trimmed beard, he revealed a chiselled face that had once been obscured by overgrown hair. His fashion even underwent changes from the oversized torn shirts and dirty pants to a fitting simple black shirt and brown pants that properly displayed his well-built physique.

"You ... cooked," she choked out trying to fill up the silence as they ate. Was it always this hard to make conversations with Dalu in the past? What was with this unspoken tension?

He nodded smiling, "Yes... I see no reason in leaving that to you all the time when I can," he supplied.

"I... it..." The spoon in her hands dropped on the floor and her eyes widened at her fidgeting. She attempted to get it at the same time that Dalu also bent which resulted in both of them bumping their heads. A moment passed where an awkward silence washed over them, and then they burst out laughing. He stood up and went to retrieve another spoon, which he handed back to her.

"We literally knocked sense into each other, right?" he asked grinning and her breath caught.

Simdi blushed nodding, "I see what you did there...nice." Her reply was followed by soft chuckles. She felt better now that they had broken the uneasiness tonight.

They ate in comfortable silence occasionally making small talk over their meal. In spite of this, the one thing they did not speak about was the kiss or the fact that Simdi was yet to explain why she reacted the way that she did three days ago. Neither of them wanted to break this collaborative air between them.

*

Next Day

It was a rainy day that morning as grey skies dampened the whole village with muddied grounds and a frigid atmosphere.

As the rain beat down on the roof heavily, Dalu who was crouched in front of the open door covered in his worn raincoat, boots, and absolutely no conviction to enter into the wet weather sighed in reluctance at the thought of braving through this rain. Beside him, Simdi held his umbrella for him while he packed his sculptures into a waterproof polyester bag after he had carefully folded them in brown paper wrappers to protect them from the rain. He was going to *Ngene* town to meet a buyer from the big city, so he could not avoid the rain. He turned to see a worried look on Simdi's face even when she knew that he would be safe. He almost smiled at the thought that she was worried about him; it touched him. It was a long time since anyone cared about him enough to worry.

"I will be fine; I know my way around. It is just a little rain..." he assured her accepting the umbrella she gave him.

"You call this little?" she asked pointing at the rain outside.

He shrugged finally standing to his full height. Even though she was taller than most women, he still towered over her. He looked down at her face etched in worry and when she caught him looking, she shyly averted her gaze. It amused him that this feisty strong young woman could still feel shy in his presence. In a way, this pleased him. He told himself that until she got over her admiration of him, he would secretly relish in these cherished moments.

"It is nothing. I told you that I do business outside and for a while, I have been neglecting it but if I do not go... Well, would you prefer it if we do not eat as well as we have been doing? The rice, the beef, the chicken, the bread, the tea...."

She rolled her eyes at him, "you'd miss it more than I would" she pointed out accusingly.

He chuckled, smirking at her. "What can I say? I am a man of fine tastes." Yes, yes, he was flirting with her even if she did not catch on to him doing it.

She blew air in between her teeth, "alright I get your point. Be safe," she muttered grudgingly.

Coming closer, he patted her short curly afro; her hair and its fast growth was another wonder to him. "Be safe too and do not venture too far. Promise me?"

She grinned impishly, "You know I won't but if it would lessen your worries to hear me say it then I won't. You better not catch a cold, I'm bad at nursing" she warned sternly.

He returned her grin, stepping outside after already opening his umbrella. When he entered the rain, he turned once more to wave at her before walking down the right path of the road until his back disappeared.

*

It was very sunny now that the rain had subsided; in its departure was the significant smell of dust mixing together with air.

Simdi sat on the little stool inside the kitchen pounding fresh pepper and ginger cloves. Most of the wood used for the cooking were wet from the rain, but she was lucky to have found some dry ones inside Dalu's workshop. A small smile found its way to her face at the thought of Dalu. Their relationship was changing right before her very eyes, since that night. He helped her with the chores and after that, they would speak of little things that went from how the weather was, to his sculptures and amusingly to his dog. She insisted that the dog should have a name and end its nameless existence. That particular conversation had been very funny.

"Why isn't your dog named?" she demanded, stroking the brown fur of the dog.

"I never bothered to name it," replied Dalu in a calm voice as he continued fixing the broken end of the centre table in the sitting room.

"How long have you had it?" she added finally looking at him.

"Do you always talk so much?" he asked tersely. For all his talkativeness when the need arose, Simdi discovered that Dalu did not like conversations. He preferred working in silence or sitting in silence.

"Oh, come on Dalu don't be annoyed. Do you always evade questions?" she asked playfully. He could not help but laugh. Dalu had one of best laughter sounds she had ever heard, a rich husky tone that never failed to impress her. It made her feel special knowing that she was the one responsible for that sound.

He shrugged finally looking at the dog. "I have had her for a long time. She was a puppy when Oyiri brought her home one afternoon." By the soft tone that his voice took, she knew immediately that Oyiri was one of his dead sons.

She cleared her throat deciding that she would not let him dwell in sorrow. "I still think you should name it, try it." She could not help but coo at the dog who opened its eyes and barked happily as if it could tell that she was the subject of their conversation.

"Dog from now on I name you *nkita*." The seriousness of which Dalu used in saying it even though there was an amused glint in his dark eyes made Simdi burst into another bout of laughter. He grinned returning his attention back to fixing the table leg.

"Isn't that still dog ... in *Igbo* language?" she pointed out.

Dalu nodded slyly, "It is better than nothing. Beggars cannot be choosers Simdi."

Simdi was brought out of her musings when the dog barked continuously. Immediately she became alert of her surroundings. She covered her already boiled porridge, and carefully moved to peek out of the small door.

Emerging from the midst was a figure. A tall woman with shoulder-length braided grey hair packed behind her head. She had a striking face, light brown skin, and she wore a disarming smile. In one hand she held a large nylon bag while she used the other to hold up her skirt in an attempt to avoid mud splatters. Simdi immediately dropped half her guard as she saw the friendly smile that the woman directed at her.

"Good day," greeted the woman when she saw Simdi approaching her.

Simdi hurried to help her with the bags as they both walked into the house. As she walked past Simdi, she noticed that the woman limped slightly. She offered her a seat and then left in search of some light refreshment. On her return, Simdi wondered about the woman who sat quietly resting from the long walk. This was the first time anyone besides Dalu's father-in- law had actually visited. It naturally made Simdi curious about who she was.

"Are you the girl that Dalu saved that night?" asked the woman by way of conversation. Simdi looked up quietly not knowing what to say. Dalu always seemed not to trust an outsider, and that was made obvious by how he always warned her to stay indoors any time any stranger passed or came along.

"Yes, I am," she confessed in a cautious voice.

A sincere smile graced the woman's face. "Please relax, I mean you no harm. I have only good intentions where Dalu is concerned, and now they extend to you also. What is your name?" she asked her again.

Simdi nodded, "I am Simdi to those who know me."

The woman gave her an approving smile before tapping her knee, "Well my captivating Simdi, I am Dalu's adoptive mother Nwakaego," announced the woman looking straight at her with knowledgeable eyes.

This was the woman who Dalu revealed to her on some nights ago had saved him from starving when his parents died. She was the only comforter whom Dalu also revealed had been his only comforter during the period when the burden of early marriage had overwhelmed him. She was also the reason why Dalu still entered into the main town to buy foodstuff.

Without thinking, Simdi clasped her hands in Nwakaego's and smiled widely at her, "thank you for everything you have done for him. Please what do I serve you?" she asked standing up.

The surprise was evident on Nwakaego's face at Simdi's words and welcoming behaviour. "Anything" she replied, her face holding a smile to show how pleased she was.

Unknown to Simdi, this very request held a lot of significance to Nwakaego because no one had ever offered her anything since the last six years she had visited here. In a way, it signified that life was finally in the home that had lost so much.

10

Meet the Parents...

*Y*our food is delicious," praised Nwakaego eating her porridge in absolute delight. She grinned when Simdi dished out more for her.

Simdi who appeared to be very flustered from all the praises she was receiving from Nwakaego shook her head humbly, "It's nothing at all."

Nwakaego shook her head in disagreement. They were both sitting on the dining table eating quietly. "It's something child. No wonder Dalu rarely enters the village anymore." A sad expression passed her face at the mention of Dalu, but it was quickly hidden. Being the observative person she was, Simdi saw it.

Discretely, she stole glances at the woman as she sipped her cup of water. "Does Dalu make you sad?" It was a question she had to ask no matter how straightforward it was.

Nwakaego observed her for a while and then suspended her eating to contemplate the question.

"That boy... he deserves more than he is given, to watch him suffer for so long saddens me."

Simdi listened in understanding; she too had witnessed the sadness that surrounded Dalu even till now. She offered Nwakaego a small grin in an attempt at reassurance. "I think if you saw him now, you would see that he's changed for the better. He eats, baths, and sleeps frequently. He's not entirely the man he was before."

Nwakaego's eyes brightened in awe, "I have to see it myself to believe this. Tell me that this is not a joke?"

Simdi shook her head confidently, "I promise you that your heart will be less worried when you set your eyes on him."

Nwakaego gave her a broad smile and then continued eating. After their food was consumed, Simdi began arranging all the foodstuff that Nwakaego brought along with her.

"How did you manage to bring all these here? I hope it was not too much to carry alone?" asked Simdi in concern.

Nwakaego who sat just outside the kitchen shook her head, "My sales attendant helped me. I sent her back to tend to the shop... I could not come a few days ago ..."

Simdi sighed in sadness, and halted her task of setting the items in their places, "the memorial of his wife's death?"

Nwakaego nodded and then looked at her in surprise, "he told you about Kaima?"

Simdi smiled forlornly remembering that torturous night when she had almost collapsed from worry at what Dalu might do to himself. "We sat down outside and drank to her memory. He loved her... very much. I think more than ever what hurts him is the fact that he is left alone to bear their loss and remember them."

She came out and sat beside Nwakaego who stared afar with a doleful expression on her face. "I didn't think that he would ever confide in anyone again, but that goes to show you that you can never underestimate the lure of companionship." She turned back to Simdi, "Would you like to know more about Dalu?" she offered cryptically.

Simdi considered her offer carefully; it was tempting but she decided against it. "The thing that I have learnt about Dalu since my time here is that Dalu hates it when it's not him who tells his story, and we just recently started getting along so..."

Nwakaego shook her head in understanding, "For you to say this shows the depth of which you have come to understand him. Instead, I want to hear about you."

What could Simdi tell her that would not sound alarming or farfetched? "I owe Dalu my life... I was running away that night... from assailants," she revealed partially twisting the truth. "Before then, I was already sick and weak. It was dark, and I didn't even see the snake. The next thing I knew was that I was burning up and then I fell unconscious. Dalu brought me here and treated me. It was not easy being with him at first because of how untrusting I was towards people. He was the only person who never seemed to push me for an explanation." She stopped her story to peel the tangerines which Nwakaego had brought along.

"Dalu is an only child," revealed the woman after a while. "He learnt from a young age about the value of space. His parents were wonderful people. His father *Uoku* was a healer and his mother *Nneoma* was a street performer... we were childhood friends. By now I'm sure that you are aware of the discrimination Dalu has faced all his life because of his mother who was an *osu*. Dalu's parents gave him all the affection that was possible. They trained him well, making sure that he was educated even when all he knew how to do was sculpt wood. I can say without a doubt that Dalu never pressed on about you because that was how he grew up. Nneoma my friend was a private woman and she would have instilled the same ideologies in her son."

It made sense looking at it from that perspective, Dalu never insisted she tell him all her secrets because he understood the value of secrets. His mother taught him so...

"Dalu's parents...what happened to them?" This was one thing she did not know. Despite how many times Dalu spoke of his childhood, he never spoke of the death of his loved ones. Neither had she, but she was curious. Was it so harrowing that he never wanted to revisit that memory?

When Nwakaego spoke this time her lips trembled, "Nneoma my friend was exquisite; in his own way Dalu inherited that trait. No matter how he looks, or what he does and says; there has always been this graceful allurement that draws people to him like flies.

Sometimes I feel that it is his reason for living so poorly over the years. He began to hate that people noticed him like they did his mother. Her beauty was so captivating that men vied for her even after she married Uoku. It was what eventually led to their tragedy."

*

Dalu was not eavesdropping. He was in his home and just happened to overhear a conversation concerning him. Why was he not moving towards them? What was this need to see Simdi's reaction to his origins? Of all the questions she could ask, she had chosen the one that he could never bring himself to ever answer no matter how hard he tried. The events of that day were forever burnt in his mind.

Sixteen years was the age a lot of things began to change in Dalu's life. He was taking on more responsibilities in the home and aiding father actively in his business. Through the little money he acquired from his sculptures, it enabled him to purchase fine ornaments for his mother and scholarly books for his father. He could feel the pride in them each time he returned from his sales. Some days he engaged in hunting and returned with meat they feasted on at night; it was a good year for them. His father stopped going to the caves because he had Dalu now. Although they were a small family, Dalu always appreciated the fact that his parents loved him and themselves irrespective of the hardships they faced in the village. It was because of this that he grew to be more serious-minded than his peers.

On that fateful day, everything had started like usual; easy and quickly ending. "My son, luck is upon us, the rabbit you caught is even fatter than most goats" praised his father proudly.

Dalu grinned happily, holding the dead animal securely on the stick it was tied to. They were returning from their visits to the caves. His father had insisted on joining him because he was feeling irrelevant from all the resting, he took nowadays. As they approached their house, a shiny white Volkswagen came into their view. It was common knowledge that only the richest of people in Umi drove such a vehicle. It was parked in front of their home and it looked so out of place. Knowing that they knew no friend that rich made them wary of the guest that was inside their house at the moment.

"Mama!" he called out dropping the rabbit unceremoniously on the ground, as he rushed

inside when he got no response. The living room was in disarray, and it made both of them more worried.

"Where is she?" demanded his father worriedly on entering into the house and seeing the state of disarray it was left in.

They heard struggling sounds of two people coming from the back of the house. Dalu looked at his father solemnly before dashing outside to rescue his mother. When he reached where the noise was concentrated, he saw his mother lying helpless on the ground; her mouth was covered with the palm of a man who forcefully tried to restrain her from screaming. Dalu went berserk at that moment, he did not hesitate as he pounced on the man which succeeded in freeing his mother. Nneoma quickly rushed to her husband with a bloodied nose and bruised lips.

The assailant was a sturdy man, who wore a blue cotton shirt and plain black trousers. On his wrist was an expensive watch, while his black glossy shoes practically screamed attention to his obvious wealth. He was a dark brown skinned man with a bald head, well-groomed goatee, and surrounded by a pompous air around him. As they tussled on the ground, it was obvious that the man was stronger than Dalu who was still lanky from puberty and weighed less. He was easily overpowered after a few minutes of struggling with the stranger.

Standing triumphantly the man spat on the sand, his eyes roving over his mother lustfully and darkening when they landed on Uoku. "How much will it cost Uoku? I want her as a second wife, tell me and I will pay. Just name your price," demanded the man looking at Dalu's father enviously. His arrogance made him foolish enough to believe that he could buy a woman greatly loved by her husband.

Uoku walked towards him and punched him so hard that the man spat out blood this time. "You think Nneoma is an object that you can buy? How dare you insult her this way? You have five seconds to leave my house, I will not be held responsible for what happens afterwards." Each one of them remained quiet because none had ever seen the gentle soft-spoken healer this furious in his life.

Dalu stood up although he staggered slightly and shouted angrily at the man, "You heard my father you he-goat! Take your fancy rubbish and leave us!"

The man continued to watch them darkly with blood on his lips, sand on his clothes and his hands clenched in anger. Even though there was hesitation in his eyes, he turned and left. Something about the deliberate way that he looked back made them know within their hearts that he would cause them trouble. No arrogant man would pull out from a fight so willingly without having something sinister up his sleeves.

*

Dalu's insecurities won over his resolve to listen and he cleared his throat to announce his presence. They had been so engrossed in discussing him that they did not hear when he entered. He looked at Nwakaego who was staring at him with her eyes bugged out and her mouth wide open.

"*Nne nwa*, you look like you have seen a ghost," he said casually looking at her briefly and then moving his attention to Simdi who approached him and collected his now empty polyester bag.

"Welcome back," she whispered only to him before asking, "I take it your client was pleased?" Dalu did not stop the shy smile that formed on his lips at her inquiry. He nodded and took the seat she had been occupying. "I will be inside if you guys need anything. Please call for me before mama Nwaka leaves okay," she said departing into the house and giving them privacy.

Dalu turned towards Nwakaego with a displeased look on his handsome face, "I thought we agreed that if I needed anything, I would come to you and not the other way around," he said accusingly.

Nwakaego who had recovered from her initial shock at his appearance scoffed unrepentantly, "I would have died of old age waiting for you then." Sighing loudly, she looked towards the path that led to the graves of his wife and children. "I know how you get during that day. I could not be there for you, but it seems that... I worried for nothing. That child Simdi, she has managed to do what I could not all these years."

Dalu did not reply to her praise and instead addressed the other issue, "you know I hate meddling. I do not need anyone sharing my stories. You should not have told her about my parents..."

Nwakaego looked heavenwards and smiled sadly, "I offered her you know, I offered her the chance to know about you and she said she would rather hear it from you because she knew you hated 'meddling' as you put it. Also, I didn't really tell her anything, you interrupted before I could."

They did not speak again as Nwakaego continued to look up to the sky while Dalu closed his eyes to rest from the journey he had made. When he opened them, he met Nwakaego's dark eyes smiling happily at him; they were filled with tears. He returned it with a warm smile of his; she was the only person left in his life who would never intentionally hurt him. Nwakaego was ... *constant*.

***

Simdi was inside her room mending her dress when he entered after seeing Nwakaego off.

"What happened?" he asked her. Dalu was waiting for her attitude to change towards him. He would not be surprised if she treated him with pity. Surprisingly he was met with a warm inviting smile.

"I was stealing dried logs from your workshop since the rain wet the others outside and my dress caught on your slicer...it's something I can fix. Have you eaten?" she asked in concern.

He nodded still not entering fully inside the room, "Yes, thank you for the delicious meal Simdi. Could you come out for a second?" he asked, and she carefully placed her dress on the bed.

"Sure...is everything okay?" she inquired following him outside to the small dimly lit living room area.

He went to where the polyester bag was placed and rummaged through it before handing her a wrapped parcel. "You said you... draw and I have artists in my ... shop so well I got this. It is obvious that you are starting to get bored without any television or radio to keep you company here."

Simdi collected the parcel and opened it eagerly. It was a medium-sized widespread drawing pad and a few coloured pencils. She looked excited and utterly shocked at this gesture. He waited for her to speak but instead, she sat on the cushioned chair opposite him and opened the drawing pad.

"This is... what I mean to say is... thank you for your thoughtfulness...would you believe that since I came here, I have never thought of drawing?" she asked in disbelief. "When I was young there were rules that I had to keep and a place I had to always be at... I never remembered anything afterwards, but I would have these dreams that showed me what my eyes could not see. I ... know I'm not making any sense, but drawing was the only way I could remember because if I ever forgot, I would never have remained as I am now." She turned to him smiling, "Honestly I have missed drawing. Surprisingly, since I came into this warm house; I found out that I have not desperately tried to preserve my memories through sketching. I doubt if I will ever forget you, or the happiness and peace I have felt since I decided to stay a little longer," she confessed gesturing towards him and the room. "Thank you for putting me into consideration."

Her honest words touched Dalu, and he found himself smiling sheepishly. He was very pleased that he took the initiative to buy the drawing materials for her, "so what will you fill it with?" he asked curiously, and she clucked her tongue already starting to sketch something.

"I think it's a more like a 'who;' it's someone I have always wanted to show you but never could," she admitted and then focused on drawing.

Dalu stretched languidly and spoke after silence had filled the room. "Thank you for refusing to hear about me from anyone other than me," he said tiredly as he burrowed closer into the cushioned chair. "There is actually no mystery to it Simdi...my father was murdered by one of my mother's ardent admirers, and my mum driven by the guilt and grief committed suicide. It is not something to proudly disclose to anyone."

It still hurt remembering it, the dead look in his mother's eyes as she walked away that morning without turning back to look at him. He had begged her so desperately to stay with him, but her mind was made up. Dalu would have given anything in this world to prevent that day if he had known it would result to the discovery of her lifeless body dangling from one of the trees inside the herb field where he and his father visited. Why had he not followed her when she said she needed time to grasp the reality that his father was dead? He believed he was doing her a favour after all they had been through on the day his father died. How wrong he had been.

His throat caught when he felt her warm fingers cover his and when he looked up, she was looking at him as if he had told her the secret to immortality. "Dalu...only very few people would experience all you have and still show kindness to others," she pointed out sincerely. At her honest words, his eyes closed instinctively because he was afraid that if he left them open, she would see too much. The silence, her determined face, and the contentment in his heart were all Dalu needed as he fell into a dreamless nap.

*

Gentle taps woke him up an hour later and he yawned looking at Simdi who returned his gaze amusedly. "This journey must have taken more from you than you let on," she observed while handing him the drawing sheet.

Dalu nodded and then looked down into the sheet. It was the face of a beautiful woman with kind eyes and refined features. She used the pencil in such a way that it conveyed the softness in this woman. "Your mother?" he asked already knowing that he was right.

Simdi exhaled loudly and leaned back into the chair letting her head fall back as she spoke. "I never knew my birth parents. This wonderful woman adopted me, and she became a mother as no other could ever compare. Till today I don't know what led to my birth or why I never met my real mother. When I asked my *nne*, she said the greatest gift she could give me was never knowing the circumstances that led to my birth.

For so long I questioned why I was the way I was... my hair, my skin colour, and my eyes. I was so different from everyone and even though I was treated like some type of sacred object, I knew of the hate that people held for me. Only my *nne* loved me, she went against all the rules to keep me, for me to have a normal life." Her voice sounded so broken and she did not look at him anymore. She was observing the ants crawling out of the small cracks on the wall.

There was a sigh and then she continued, "Do you remember when you told me that I was bitten by a snake...? You must have questioned why I looked surprised that you thought I would die... for so long, I have always been indestructible," she finished laughing at a joke only she understood.

"No one is indestructible Simdi," he pointed out and she finally looked at him giving him a hard look.

"I am Dalu." She stopped and sighed before speaking, "This body... this beautiful body... I have hated this body since I can remember because I grew up with the constant reminder that it was being prepared for something far more incomprehensible."

Dalu could hear the vehemence in her voice and it did not make any sense why she would disassociate herself from a body she was born with.

"Remember when I cut myself...what I told you...I said it would be gone before you knew it," she reminded him as a matter of fact and stood. She approached him uncertainly and he sat up attentively. Slowly she raised the sleeves of her dress and began untying the bandages he used to cover the cuts she had inflicted on herself. Dalu gawked at her with a stunned countenance fixed on his face. Before his very eyes, the cuts had faded and in their place were barely visible lines. She pushed down the neckline of her dress to show that the stab wound had disappeared as well.

"How is this possible?" he asked her as he stood and moved to hold her shoulder while his hands trailed down her left arm quizzically.

Simdi's despondent hazel iris stared into his dark brown eyes. "If you are wise, you would tell me to leave now and never come back."

"Simdi..." he tried saying as he looked down at her. Why could he not speak? Was it because of the transparency in her words, the raw conviction that challenged him? Dalu was afraid suddenly of Simdi but it was not because of this revelation. This girl with her innocent smiles and resilient nature could break him far worse than death and grief had. The ironic part of it was that he was starting to see that if that was what she intended to do, Dalu would let her.

***

With the revelation of part of her true nature, she expected Dalu to send her packing but instead he gathered her in his arms offering her the physical comfort she had cluelessly not known that she craved. She tried escaping the embrace out of embarrassment and the fact that she felt very imperfect, but he held on undeterred.

"Why? Why must you go so far for me?" she demanded, hating how her voice trembled. Finally, she stopped struggling and held onto him afraid that if she did not, she would fall. It felt good, she realized; it felt amazing relying on someone else other than herself. She felt weightless at telling him this much. It was like he was accepting part of her burden and claiming it as his own. Her heart clenched at his warmth; this man Dalu...*she realized instantly that she wanted him; she wanted to be with him for as long as it took.*

They spent the rest of the night seated quietly in the living room as she explained exactly what it meant to be the vessel of the river goddess, and the rules she must break to remain free of her control.

Simdi knew within herself that things would only get harder as she progressed in this new life that she had escaped into, but as she sat there in the cosy living room in the arms of this one man who had changed all his flaws just to bridge the gap between them; she knew that they would be fine. The hopeful part of her also anticipated the remaining days to come and what path this new found feeling between them would lead them towards. Were they ready? No, the right question here was if she was ready to love this man with everything she had?

For now, her race was paused, and another pace had been set. A new journey where she would set herself free had already begun and she would fight with all that was within her to have a future with this man whom she wanted to stay with more than anything else in the world.

To Be Continued......

Glossary

- Abacha   Eastern delicacy made from Tapio

- Ada   Term used for First born Daughter in Eastern Nigeria

- Afuna   Once you have seen the father

- Akajiego   The hand that controls money

- Akidi   Native Beans

- Amah   Surname

- Bia fu   Come and See

- Chikaima   Only God we know (Nickname:- Kaima)

- Chinasa   God Replies

- Chinedu   God leads or God guides

- Chisimdi   God said I should be (Nickname:- Simdi)

- Daluchukwu   Thank God (Nickname:- Dalu)

- Ejim   Surname

- IGBO   Eastern Tribe in Nigeria

- Ifeanyi   Our own

- Imo   State in Eastern Nigeria

- Isi owu   Thread tied hair

- Jellof Rice   Popular rice dish in Nigeria

- Mazi   Traditional Abbreviation for Mr.

- Ndi mmiri   River people

- Ngene Town   Fictional Village

- Ndubisi   Life is most important or Obedience
- Nkechi   God's own

- Nkita   Igbo way of Pronouncing Dog

- Nkoli   Merriment

- Nne   Igbo Term for Mother

- Nwakaego   A child is more valuable than money
- Nwayo   Take it easy

- Nzu   Traditional chalk

- Obinna   Father's heart

221

- Obi m — My heart

- Ogechi — God's Time

- Ogene — Traditional Gong

- Okorie — Male born on the traditional market day

- Onwu — Death

- Onwummiri — River of Death

- Onyeji — Who hold

- Onye ara — Mad man

- Osu/ Osu a — Outcast/ This outcast

- Otangele — Traditional eye pencil in Igboland

- Oyirinnaya — His father's replica   (Nickname:- Oyiri)

- Taanua — Today

- Tochi — Praise God

- Uche — Though(s)

- Udenta — At the appointed time

- Ugo — Prestige

- Ujumwa   Child born in a time of sorrow

- Umeh   Surname

- Umi   Fictional village (Sweet Nectar)

- Uoku   Fictional name that does not exist

- Uzo   The way or the path

About the Author

Ruth Anthony-Obi is a Nigerian fiction writer who has had a knack for writing since the age of six.

She studied Mass Communication at Enugu State University of Science and Technology (ESUT) and obtained a Masters' degree in Media and Journalism from Newcastle University, United Kingdom.

Her work was created solely to inspire people while giving a face and character to different topics prevalent in African culture and society through fictious storytelling.

Creatures of Fate Trilogy is an expanded and revised version of her first published work in 2014.

She actively immerses in story writing through her social media pages on Facebook: "*the Nigerian Storyteller*" and her Instagram writing page: *@theword_spinner*. Ruth is currently working on more exciting pieces to share with her readers.

Printed in Great Britain
by Amazon